A
PLACE
OF
LIGHT

A
PLACE
OF
LIGHT

Stories

Mary Bush

William Morrow
and Company, Inc.
New York

The author is grateful for permission to reprint stories that appeared,
sometimes in slightly different form, in the following publications:
Black Warrior Review ("Muskrat"), *Missouri Review* ("A Place of Light"),
Plainswoman ("Rude Awakening"), *Sing Heavenly Muse* ("Cure"), and
Syracuse Scholar ("Difficult Passage").

Library of Congress Cataloging-in-Publication Data

Bush, Mary, 1949–
    A place of light / Mary Bush.
      p.   cm.
    ISBN 0-688-06255-5
    I. Title.
  PS3552.U8215P55   1989
  813'.54—dc20   89-36151
                                                                      CIP

Printed in the United States of America

First Edition

1 2 3 4 5 6 7 8 9 10

BOOK DESIGN BY RICHARD ORIOLO

In gratitude
to my two teachers,
George P. Elliott
and
Raymond Carver

CONTENTS

CURE

We did not have the carp tail, but we did have the skull of a mole and the brown clay. If we could get the carp by supper, then leave the tail to dry, in the morning our mother would be sitting up and she would be all right. The mole we took away from the cat. The clay we got from swimming where the houses are being built, where they are digging the cellars. The only place for carp is the canal.

Great-aunt Maria strained tea wearing one black glove. She had the wad of parsley stuck up one nostril, part of it starting to fall out. It was the special parsley, that grew wild, the kind that kept away disease. She is the one who told us about the carp, the mole, and the clay.

Our father cried when the doctor left, hiding his face, and quiet so we would not know. Our mother was never sick before, never. But now it was the fifth day that she lay in bed, with the doctor coming almost every day and Great-aunt Maria coming to make tea and say prayers and cook for us. They would not let my brother and me in there, and they did not tell us anything except Quiet and Go outside and play and You, girl, watch your brother. But when we saw father crying we decided she was going to die. Then Great-aunt Maria said she could make a poultice, but father said, "There will be no voodoo in this house. We believe in doctors in this house."

So Maria would say her prayers in those words we could not understand while she made tea or washed dishes or cooked for us. When father was gone she would say, "All your mama needs is the Cure. Carp mole clay." But she did not talk looking at us. She talked into pots and cups so that we could hear her but so that she was not telling us.

She told the pots and cups exactly how to make it, where to get the things, and when to get them. She told the pots and cups when our father was not there, and we heard her and looked at each other. And Father would come in and say, "Good Christ, Maria, it's the middle of August, take off that glove." Or he would look at her and say, "Some day you are going to take a deep breath and suffocate on that weed." And she would make tea or wash dishes or cook for us, saying her prayers, without looking at anyone.

Now our father did not care anymore where we were because all he did was sit with her and wait for the doctor and tell Maria to take off her glove. We took our poles, and my brother took the knife from the kitchen. When Maria's back was turned I got the matches from the stove.

I was bigger, so I pedaled and he sat on the handlebars and we both held the poles. We hid the bike under the bushes and walked down Main Street. In front of the diner is the best place. We found four or five butts between the street and curb, most of them almost too short to hold, and my brother found a piece of cigar with a plastic holder and the teeth marks on it. Then Meltzer yelled You Kids from the front of his store and we ran around the corner. We passed the A & P and headed back down to the canal.

We used the knife to dig under the elderberry bush where it was damp, but the worms were all skinny and little. Then we dug down near the water where the bank had caved in and you could touch the water but there was nothing there. So we had to use the skinny ones. Nobody else was fishing except way down on the bridge there was one kid with a pole. We watched him pull on his line and lean over and sit down and wait and pull again. When it broke he left.

Then we took them out and I hit a match on a stone and lit us both up. "How's yours?" I asked.

"Pretty good," he said.

I told him, "You're going to share that cigar with me."

"I don't know yet," he said.

"It's my bike," I told him.

We smoked and waited for some bites. He said, "You think we are going to be like the Allen kids?"

"I don't know," I told him. I could see he was scared.

"There's four of them," he said. "And only their father takes care of them. He cooks, too."

"I know," I said.

He got a bite. His worm was gone, so he put a new one on. I was getting hot, and my T-shirt was sticking to me. I put my hand under the shirt and stretched the cloth with my fist, to pull the shirt away from my chest. He looked at me.

"You are too getting them," he said. "You said you wasn't getting them, but you are."

"I am not," I said, and I sat up straight and pulled at the shirt to make them go away.

"They're big, too," he said.

"Shut up, ass," I told him.

Then we smoked the cigar.

We stayed a long time getting nibbles, losing our worms, and we finished all the butts.

"What we going to do if we don't catch one?" my brother asked.

"We'll get one," I told him. Then I said, "You stay here and watch my pole."

"We gotta go home pretty soon," he said. "And we don't have a carp. If we don't get one—"

I stood there looking at him and I couldn't tell what brown was from the sun and what brown was from the dirt. I knew he was going to cry.

"If we don't get one," he said.

"Shut up," I told him. "Shut up and watch the poles or we won't catch anything."

I put the knife in the waist of my pants and walked along the bank, careful not to step on twigs or make a sound, making my face go hard because I was White Falcon, the warrior, I was strong and I did not care about anything. I was looking for a place to dig worms. I passed a tangled piece of line and a half-rotted sunfish, an old Coke bottle, a branch stuck in the ground to hold a pole.

Then I saw him down near the other bridge, the shape

I knew that was Ed Otts. I kept walking because I was not afraid of anything. He put his bag down and looked at me. He coughed and spit into the canal. Then I was near him and I saw there were two fish on the ground behind him and his pole, too, was on the ground. One of the fish was a carp.

I ran back to my brother and told him, "Old Man Otts is down by the other bridge catching carp." We grabbed our poles and the skinny worms we had put on the burdock leaf, and we took off.

We went as close to him as we dared and we put our lines in. He kept coughing and spitting and we could tell he was looking at us. I sat up straight and stretched the shirt away from my body.

After a while he said, "What you kids fishing for?"

"Carp," I told him, watching my line.

We fished for a while. I pulled in a sunfish. "We gotta go," my brother said to me with that crying sound. We kept fishing with old Ed Otts watching us.

"I got a carp right here," Ed Otts told us. "Going to throw it back in."

We stopped fishing and looked at him. "We'll take that carp if you don't want it," I told him.

He looked down toward the other bridge. "What you want with a carp," he said.

"We're going to eat it," I told him.

He looked at me a long time, then at my brother, then back at me. "I can see you ain't no niggers," he said. "You must be wops if you planning to eat carp."

We didn't say anything.

He picked up his pole and played with the hook that was stuck in the handle. Then he put it down. "That ain't my carp anyways," he said. "Somebody else left that carcass here. Take it if you want."

We stood up. I went behind Ed Otts and bent over to get the fish. It was a big one, and I saw that it had been dead some time. "It's rotten," I said. "It stinks." Then I felt him close behind me, and I turned quick, jumping away from his hand. I looked at him. His eyes were wet and pushed into his face. When he opened his mouth I saw that broken tooth.

I kept moving away. "Get the poles," I told my brother. I picked up my own pole and reeled it in.

"I can't," he said, with that crying sound. "It's caught." He was tugging at his line, and then he was fighting it.

"I got something," he said.

"Snap your line," I told him. "Reel in."

"It's a big one," he said, jerking his pole, reeling the line.

He pulled the fish in, and I grabbed at it. He held his pole while I held the fish with the line in its mouth.

Then we both started walking away fast, with Old Man Otts watching. I could still feel the place on my back where he touched me. He coughed and spit and called to us. "Big girl like you oughta wear a bra," he said. Then we ran.

When we got back to the bike we dropped the poles and the fish. "It's a carp," my brother said. The fish was big and shiny. It worked its mouth, and twisted its tail as it flopped on the grass. I put my foot on its side to hold it still and tried to get the hook out. But the hook was deep in the fish's throat. I worked at it while the fish stared and gasped and tried to twist away. Blood trickled from its mouth.

"It won't come out," I said. "He swallowed the hook." I took the knife from my pants.

"No," my brother said. "It's my last hook." Then he tried.

"Leave it," I told him. "It won't come."

"I think I've got it," he said.

The fish was wild.

"We have to go," I told my brother.

"Cut its tail off," he told me. "When it's dead I can get the hook out. It's almost out."

I watched the fish. "I can't if he's alive," I said. The fish wriggled under my brother's foot. "Let me try again," I told him.

I sat on the ground and held the fish through the gills, its body pressed between my knees. I worked my fingers into its mouth and moved the hook until I felt something crunching. I swallowed the blood taste in my own mouth, and kept at the hook until it was free.

I let the fish go and it lay on the grass breathing air, its eyes wide. "We need an ax for the tail," I told my brother. "This knife's no good. We gotta take it home and ax it."

"How we gonna get it home?" he asked.

When I told him, he said no. Then we stood there looking at the fish. We couldn't leave the poles behind. It would take too long for one of us to walk with it. It was getting late.

"Because I need more room because I'm pedaling," I told him again. "And besides, your shirt's longer."

"Okay," he finally said.

So he tucked his shirt in and we put the fish inside his shirt. Then the fish moved and he put his hand to the shirt, and his face was sick. He sat on the handlebars and we both held the poles while I rode him home.

We went right to the shed and we put the fish on the

wooden bench. Then I got the ax. But the fish still wasn't dead. It worked its mouth and flipped and then lay still until it jerked again, gasping, its eyes open wide.

"Does it hurt him?" my brother asked.

"They don't feel anything," I told him.

"He acts like it hurts," my brother said.

I squeezed the ax handle. "We should have taken that dead one," I said.

We waited for the fish to die.

"Should we kill it?" my brother asked. "Should we cut off its tail now?"

"I think it's dead," I told him. I lifted the ax. The fish flipped over, suddenly, and it fell off the bench, into the dark below. We heard it knock against the paint cans.

We dropped to our knees and looked for the fish, pushing aside rusted coffee cans full of nails, a shovel blade, and pieces of two-by-fours. It was dark, and we couldn't see or hear the fish. We felt with our hands, but touched only the cold floor, the dirt and cobwebs, scraps of wood and nails.

"I don't hear it anymore," my brother said.

"Quiet," I told him.

We listened.

"We need a flashlight," I said. "It's too dark."

"Maybe it's dead now," he whispered.

We heard the fish move again, far underneath the bench, against the cans and junk.

"We have to get a light," I told him. We waited. There were no other sounds. "He's dead," I told my brother. "Let's get the flashlight."

We left the fish and went into the house.

Doc Rouse was there. We could hear his voice in where our mother was, talking to Father. Great-aunt Maria

stirred our supper on the stove with one black glove, saying her prayers. She did not look at us.

Then Father and the doctor came out and the doctor
was saying it was the shot that finally did it. I looked at
the cupboard, wondering what kind of shot, because he
used both kinds. But then there was always that third
kind, too, like Uncle Rem and the cow he took out in
the field. They wouldn't, I thought, and I looked at my
brother and he looked at me, and we did not know what
it was the shot did.

"I thought at first," the doctor said, "those tablets
would do the trick."

Maria was saying her prayers.

"With something like this," he said, "you never know.
You just have to keep trying and hope something works.
Be thankful."

Father was wiping the hair from his forehead, looking
down at the linoleum, looking like he just got out of bed.
"I am," he said. "Yes. I am." He sounded like he was
talking in his sleep.

The doctor put his hand on Father's shoulder. "I'll
stop by in the morning and give her another shot. She'll
be up and dancing in no time." He nodded at Father and
slapped him there on his shoulder.

Then Father looked at us and his face changed like he
finally woke up. "Good Christ," he said. "What the hell's
on you? What is that?"

From fishing, we told him.

He grabbed my brother and shook him, saying,
"Christ Almighty."

"Daddy," my brother said, and he let go.

"Couple of little rascals, eh?" the doctor said. He left,
walking past Maria stirring our supper with one black

glove. She looked at me. When our eyes met, her head dropped, like she was going to nod. But she didn't nod. She just stood there with her head down. Then she turned back to her pot.

"I should beat the living hell out of both of you," Father said. But he sat down and put his head in his hands like he would cry again, or else fall asleep. All we could hear was the scrape scrape of Maria stirring our supper and her old voice mumbling those words that we did not understand.

"Wash up," he told us. "Wash up and change those goddamn clothes. Then go in there and see your mother."

OUTLAWS

This time her Uncle Jo Jo had a rusty brown station wagon parked in his driveway, the hood up, his toolbox open on the lawn.

When Josie and her mother pulled in behind the station wagon, Uncle Jo Jo came out of the house. He stood on the top step and raised his coffee mug in the air. "Hey, pardner," he called out.

Josie knew she was his favorite. Sometimes after he finished working on a car he'd take her with him on a test run. They'd drive out on the muck roads and he'd shout,

"Let her rip," then hit the gas, and they'd spin off down the road, hooting and throwing up a trail of dust, with Josie steering.

Josie's mother drummed her fingers on the dashboard. "Hurry up," she said. "I'll be late for work."

That wasn't true, anyway, Josie thought. Her mother cooked the specials at the diner and could go in anytime around nine she wanted.

Uncle Jo Jo came down the steps and stood near the station wagon. He grinned at them while Josie's mother kept her eyes straight ahead. She was always mad at her brother for something. She was mad that he'd disconnected the safety shield at work and had the accident. She was mad that her brother's wife, Irene, had to support the family—just like she had to. She was mad about the way Cousin Eddie turned out. Most of all, Josie thought, she was mad that Josie and her uncle had so much fun together.

"I'd be fun, too," her mother said, "if I had somebody looking after me hand and foot like I was the Dalai Lama. Irene's a worse fool than he is. Thank God they found each other."

Josie gathered her school things and slammed the car door shut. At least she'd be able to spend Teachers' Conference Day off with Uncle Jo Jo, even if she did have schoolwork to do. Her mother backed out of the driveway. She raised her fingers from the steering wheel as a good-bye, then pulled away.

Uncle Jo Jo shook his head after her.

"What's wrong with the car?" Josie asked him.

Uncle Jo Jo set his coffee mug down on the fender. "She's dying of a broken heart," he said. He sounded a little sad about it.

"Oh," Josie said.

"I've reground the cylinders," he told her. "Now I have to set the timing."

She told him about the extra-credit science project she had to turn in the next day if she wanted to pass the fourth grade. "I need twenty leaves in all," she told him. "So far I've got maple, elm, box elder, sumac, cedar, weeping willow, and birch."

"That's plenty," he said.

When she didn't say anything he told her to check the backyard. "There's lots of trees out there. There's all kinds of maples. Get more." He sounded a little annoyed, and she wondered if something was wrong. He went into the garage and came back running an extension cord. Then he went to work without saying anything else.

The backyard was bordered by tall scraggly shrubs, but she wasn't sure they counted as trees. Over behind the garden Uncle Jo Jo had started spading up his clump of dwarf fruit trees. Every year the apples and pears grew the size of her little fingernail, then died and fell off. Uncle Jo Jo sprayed them and pruned them and read books on what to do, but they still fell off. Josie wasn't sure if dwarf fruit trees were like shrubs and wouldn't count, but she plucked two leaves just the same and put them in her notebook.

She went in the back door to the kitchen and dropped her school things on the table, then started snooping for something to eat. She hadn't touched the breakfast her mother had made for her. "I'll throw up," Josie had told her.

"Fine," her mother said. "You always know what's best anyway, don't you? That's why you're going to be the first one in our family to repeat a grade. I hope you're proud."

Josie found some powdered donuts in Uncle Jo Jo's

cupboard. At least somebody knew what good food was. She cleared a place on the table, next to a pile of dirty spark plugs and a couple of grease-smudged magazines. Aunt Irene always had a fit about Uncle Jo Jo's hunting and fishing and car magazines and his books about fruit trees. She told him things would have been better all around if he'd paid half as much attention to Eddie as he did to those "pictures of oil gaskets and deer heads." She used to be okay, but lately anything anybody did was wrong. She had a line between her eyes, straight up in the air like a flagpole, worse than the one her mother had.

Josie poured herself a glass of milk and sat down to look at the pictures in the fishing magazine. But when she reached for it she noticed an opened letter, poking out from under the junk basket.

The letter was addressed to Aunt Irene and was from Cousin Eddie in New York City. After Irene's name Eddie had printed: *And Nobody Else.* Josie looked up at the doorway and listened for Uncle Jo Jo. When she heard him working on the car, she took the letter out and read it.

Eddie told Aunt Irene that his hepatitis was better and he was working out in a gym and had a part-time job, but he didn't say doing what. The weather was okay. He had to pay seventy-five cents for one lousy apple. If she still wanted to come visit, he could find her a place to stay. And thanks for the birthday card and the money.

Cousin Eddie had just turned eighteen. "He's a man now," Josie's mother said. "Too bad his father had to miss everything." Josie's mother had sent Eddie a card with five dollars, and Josie had signed her own name to it.

Josie folded the letter and put it back. Cousin Eddie was what Josie's father called a "hellion"—except when he had a pen or pencil in his hands. Then he drew real-life pictures: wrestlers straining to pin each other, or heavy-weight boxers throwing punches, the muscles in their legs and arms bulging. Uncle Jo Jo hated Eddie's drawings. He said Eddie should learn to do something useful, instead of "living in his head" or "wrecking every damn thing he laid eyes on." He told Eddie he should study to be a car mechanic, or a hotel manager, or even a salesman, anything but a bum. A lot of people said it was because of Uncle Jo Jo that Eddie turned out the way he did.

Of course, Josie knew that wasn't true. Eddie really *was* a hellion. When he was fourteen, Eddie broke into the high school with some other kids and spray-painted the halls and threw books and papers all over. Later he stole a car and almost got sent to juvenile detention. Then he ran away from home a couple times, but somebody always found him and brought him back. Now he lived in a warehouse in New York City and nobody was trying to make him come home anymore, not even Aunt Irene.

Josie knew Uncle Jo Jo felt bad about Eddie, even though he pretended not to, because one time he came over drunk when Josie was supposed to be asleep and told Josie's mother all about it. Josie sneaked out of bed and sat on the stairs to watch and listen. Jo Jo said that Eddie's hatred for him was a knife in his heart, and he didn't know how much longer he could go on. "Every time I gave him hell, every time I slapped him—don't you know I was just trying to make him turn out decent?" And then he told Josie's mother about the money he tried to send Eddie. He'd mailed it without a note or return address, and even drove to the city for the postmark so Eddie wouldn't know who it was from. Eddie returned it to him, unopened.

Josie brushed the powdered sugar from her face. It

was funny how one person could think somebody was wonderful while another person couldn't stand him. Like the way people always said Josie's mother was so friendly and nice when Josie knew the truth: that she was really a witch. Anyway, it didn't matter to her if nobody else on earth liked Uncle Jo Jo. She liked him.

As she headed for the door she wondered what it would be like to live in New York City in a warehouse. If things kept going the way they were with her mother, she thought, she might have to write to Cousin Eddie and find out.

Uncle Jo Jo was putting his tools back in the box.

"We're just about ready to roll," he told her, sounding a little more like himself. "What say we take this buggy out on the Oxbow and see what she thinks about hills?"

"I have to get leaves," she reminded him.

"Where we're going," he said, "you can get all the leaves you need just by standing in one spot and waving your arms through the air."

She followed him into the house and watched him scrub his hands at the sink. He used a special soap that came in a can and looked like the paste they used in school. It smelled awful.

He looked over at the mess she'd left on the table. "Hey," he said. "Let's pack a lunch and take it up there to eat."

She made the baloney sandwiches while he found a couple beers and a soda and half a package of Lorna Doones she hadn't seen.

Uncle Jo Jo revved the engine. He pulled out of the drive and headed for the highway. Every once in a while he stepped on the gas, then let off and listened. "Still got a little knock," he said.

The open country did something to him. When they turned onto the Oxbow road, he hit the gas. "Okay, baby, this is it," he called out.

Josie turned up the radio, and they spun along with the radio blaring "Heart of Gold."

Keep me searching for a heart of gold, they sang, *and I'm getting old.*

"We're Bonnie and Clyde," he shouted to her over the radio. They had seen the movie together, and everything they did now was from the movie. "Stick with me, kid," he said. "We're gonna outrun those Feds." He looked in the rearview mirror and pushed the gas pedal to the floor as they started up the Oxbow hill. "Whatever happens," he shouted, "remember I love you, Bonnie."

She felt warm and gushy all over when he talked like that. Josie's secret fantasy was that Aunt Irene would get cancer and die. She was always afraid she had it anyway. Then Josie would have to go live with her uncle so he wouldn't be all alone.

"Don't go off the road, Clyde," she shouted back to him.

The car barely made it up the Oxbow. "We'll just have to tell old Snyder to keep his jalopy on the flatlands," he said.

They had to park on the side of the road because the county had put a chain across the bridge to keep kids from having beer parties in there. She ducked under the chain, and he stepped over it, lifting each leg with both hands. She waited for him to catch his breath, and then they crossed the bridge.

Josie had never been there before. Right across the

bridge was a wide meadow of weeds; everything else was trees. A single bird chirped; otherwise the place was so still it was almost eerie. They took an overgrown trail that led into the woods. Uncle Jo Jo grabbed at leaves. "See what I mean?" he said, and he tossed them into the air.

They came out at the waterfall—or what used to be a waterfall. Now barely a trickle ran down the gorge, even though it was still early in the year.

"The whole world's drying up," Uncle Jo Jo told her. "Those damn scientists keep trying to tell us we'll be in trouble if the glaciers melt, but I say it'll be the best damn thing that ever happened."

"What's that tree?" she asked.

"That's a horse chestnut," he said. "Don't you know that?"

"It's not in our book."

He pointed to the creek below. "See if you can figure it out. The creek's always full and running down there, just like up at the bridge, but nothing goes over the edge." He looked at her and shrugged.

They left the lunch near the gorge and went into the woods. Uncle Jo Jo picked leaves and handed them to her. "Aspen," he said. "Beech. Chokecherry . . ." He watched as she wrote the names down in her notebook. When they came to a big spreading tree he clasped his hands together and gave her a boost up. She felt his legs wobble a little as she reached for a leaf. When the steam valve broke loose at work it shot a plug of metal right through his chest and out his back. He got a collapsed lung, a couple broken ribs, and a bruised spinal cord that put him in a wheelchair for nearly a year. Now his legs were half as strong as they used to be, and he got bronchitis all the time. He let her down. "Oak," he told her, and he watched her lay the leaf in her notebook and write its name.

"Look at this," he said. He showed her a maple leaf. "See those little brown bumps? This tree is in trouble."

She looked at the leaf, then back at him.

"It's got a disease," he said. "You can tell everything there is to know about a tree by looking at its leaves."

"I don't want to know anything," she told him. "I'm going to quit school when I'm sixteen and go on a safari to Africa."

The minute she mentioned quitting school she was sorry, but it didn't seem to bother him.

"Look at this sucker," Jo Jo said. He held up a leaf as big as his hand. "Speaking of going on a safari."

He found another and pressed one to each side of his head, then bent forward, swinging his head from side to side. "Put these in your collection," he said. "Elephant ears."

"There's no such thing."

"Make up a name," he told her. "Your teacher's not going to know what they are." He dropped the leaves and put his hands in his pockets.

"She's got a book," Josie told him.

And then, before she knew what she was doing, she blurted it out to him: "My mother's going to send me away to an institution if I don't pass." She stopped walking and looked at him.

He gave her a funny look, like he hadn't really heard what she'd said, but was trying to figure it out. "Why, that's the craziest thing I ever heard of," he told her.

"All she ever does is yell at me," Josie said. "And I'm not even failing. Except science. Do you think she'll really do it?"

Jo Jo picked a leaf from a low tree and looked at it. Then he tossed it. "She's not sending you anywhere."

"She says I'm getting just like my father."

"Is that right?" He shook his head. "I don't know."

Josie's father lived in a rented room over the barbershop because Josie's mother had "come to the end of her rope" with him. His construction business was going bankrupt, and Josie's mother was through patching things up for him. He could do it himself if he was so smart, she told him.

"It's just her female trouble," Uncle Jo Jo said. "Everything in the world is female trouble."

"She says the trouble is my father," Josie told him.

"Let's go back," he said. "There's nothing but box elder over this way." He plucked a handful of leaves. "This is one worthless tree if I ever saw one."

"I've already got that one anyway."

Uncle Jo Jo dropped the leaves and leaned back against a tree. He looked up into the branches. "Jesus," he said.

Josie thought his lungs were hurting him, from all the walking. But then he looked at her and said, "I've gotta remember to buy some glue." He shook his head. "Let's take a break," he told her.

They sat at the top of the gorge, and Uncle Jo Jo opened a beer. "Boy, that's good," he said. He took another swallow, then set the can down.

Josie lay the notebook in her lap and started flipping through the pages, counting.

"That thing looks stuffed," Jo Jo told her.

"I don't believe it," she said. "I only need one more." She looked at him. "One more and I'm finished."

"No kidding?" he said. He leaned back on his hands. "Great. That's great."

He looked out at the gorge in front of them and motioned with his head. The sky was deep blue with little puffs of clouds. Bright evergreens grew down the gorge walls and spread out in a widening valley.

"That valley runs all the way to the lake," he said.

Josie bit into her baloney sandwich. "When can we go swimming?" Uncle Jo Jo always took her once the water warmed up.

"We're going fishing this year," he told her. "As soon as I get my boat fixed, we're taking her to Dead Man's Island."

She had never been there before, although she had seen it from the beach. She had never been to *any* island. She imagined herself hiking the craggy, deserted shore, hiding out from pirates.

"What'll it be?" her uncle asked her. "The usual?" He had almost finished his beer.

"Okay," she told him. "Give me the usual."

He set the beer can down on the grass in front of her with a wink, just one more good reason why she should live with him instead of her stupid mother.

They ate everything. They finished all the Lorna Doones and lay back on the grass, looking up at the sky. Uncle Jo Jo started talking about how he was going to fix his boat. It was a little motorboat he'd bought from a friend last summer, but he still hadn't gotten it in the water. Then he told her how he'd been thinking of buying one of those giant cabin cruisers someday and "doing the Great Lakes"—like Huck Finn, only more sophisticated, he said. He'd travel the whole summer, up the St. Lawrence and through the chain of lakes, clear all the way to Duluth.

He sat up. "Jesus," he said. "What the hell do I want with a boat?" He looked around at the trees, then out at the valley. "This is such a frigging beautiful place," he said. He dropped his head in his hands. "God Almighty."

Josie sat up and looked at him.

After a while he raised his head. He looked out at the valley and shook his head, thinking. "I'm in big trouble, Little Jo," he said. He stared hard at her. "I steamed open Irene's letter from Eddie," he said, and he looked miserable.

Josie didn't see what was so awful about that. Sherlock Holmes steamed open letters. Perry Mason probably did it too. Besides, she'd read the letter herself, though she felt a little funny about it now.

"I've got a couple more of those letters I never let Irene see," Jo Jo said. "I know she knows something's up." He opened another beer and took a long swallow. "I have to glue that frigging letter shut before she comes home."

This was the most exciting news Josie had heard in a long time. She tried not to smile.

"We've got Elmer's glue at our house," she told him.

"He hates me," Jo Jo said. "They both do. They talk on the phone. She sends him things, money. Now she's gonna go visit, who knows what'll happen next? Nobody says a word to me. It's like I'm dead, like I don't exist."

He brushed his hand through the grass, as if trying to clear something away. "Do you know how that makes me feel?" he said. "The bastard."

Josie didn't know what to say. Uncle Jo Jo never talked about Cousin Eddie—unless Eddie was there and he was yelling at him, or else complaining to somebody about things Eddie had done.

"I don't know what's happening to me," Uncle Jo Jo said. "I don't know what the hell I'm doing anymore."

He took another swallow of beer and handed her the can. She looked at him, then took a sip. She set the beer can down in front of him.

"You want to know something else?" Uncle Jo Jo

said. He looked at Josie for the longest time. Then he told her: "Irene sleeps in the spare bedroom. She's been doing that three months now." He fell back on the grass. "God Almighty, I think I'm losing my mind."

She felt funny hearing him talk like that about Cousin Eddie and Aunt Irene—telling her private things. His voice sounded funny, too, like he was going to cry, and that scared her.

She tugged at blades of grass and let them drop. "You're not losing your mind," she told him.

He lay still, with his hand covering his eyes, for a long time.

Then he said, "At least you love me. Don't you?"

She looked away at the trees. "Well, sure," she answered.

He sat up again. "You're the sweetest, dearest girl in the world."

He was so serious that she felt herself blush.

"Do you want to get that leaf now?" she asked him.

"In a minute," he said. "Come sit next to me."

She looked at him, puzzled.

"Oh, Bonnie, I'm so cold," he said. "Come here and warm me up. Just for a minute."

"My science project is due tomorrow," she told him.

He clasped his hands to his chest. "They got me, Bonnie. The Feds got me." He looked down at his hands. "I'm losing blood fast. Get some bandages."

When she didn't move, he said, "Just sit next to me for a minute, till I get my bearings. Then I'll find that leaf for you."

She wasn't sure what was wrong with him, but she inched over anyway. He smiled and nodded for her to get closer.

She sat beside him and held herself still.

"Thanks, Bonnie," he said. "I'm feeling better already."

They sat together for a while. "There must be a million birds out there," he said. He sighed, listening. And then he put his arm around her shoulders.

She started to move away, but he pulled her close. "Don't go," he said.

He pulled her to his side, and she could smell the grease from the cars, and the special soap he used. He bent his face down to her neck. Josie shoved his head away and pulled free while he mumbled, "Please, Bonnie."

She stood away from him, horrified. She moved toward the woods, then stopped. She wasn't sure if she'd be able to walk home from there.

"Oh God," Jo Jo said. "God Almighty, Little Jo." He got up on his knees. "I didn't mean anything. I was playing. I didn't mean to scare you," he said.

She felt ashamed to see him on his knees and to hear him talking like that. She wished she was home. She wished her mother was there, even if all she ever did was yell.

"I was just playing," he said. "I wouldn't hurt you for anything in the world. You know that, don't you?"

She looked at him, trying to figure it out. She shrugged. "I guess so," she said.

He stood and brushed off his pants.

Josie watched him fumble as he picked up their lunch things. Maybe her imagination was just running wild, like her mother always said it did. They were playing Bonnie and Clyde—and Bonnie and Clyde did things like that.

"We better get going," he said. "We better go back." He sounded embarrassed, and she felt bad for making such a big deal out of it.

She picked up her notebook and followed him into the woods. She wished he would say something, but he walked ahead, silent. She kept her eyes on his back as they walked. Every now and then he put his hand out and touched an overhanging branch as he passed it. The sunlight flashed across his shirt, like he was breaking up into little parts that would float away into the air.

They came out at the bridge. Halfway across, Uncle Jo Jo stopped. Josie watched him from a few feet away. He leaned over the railing, the way he did when he needed to rest, and looked at the creek.

After a time he turned to her. "I don't believe this," he said, and he pointed to the water. "*Lily pads,* for Christ's sakes."

He turned back to the creek and gazed up ahead, where the water curved around the shrubs that grew along the Oxbow road. "I wonder how they got here?"

Josie went closer and strained to see over the bridge. He moved down, giving her room, and nodded. "Take a look."

At first she didn't see anything. But then she noticed the clump of round leaves floating near the bank, where he pointed.

"It doesn't make sense," he said. "You don't find lily pads in water like this. They shouldn't be here."

She'd seen pictures of them with big fat flowers, or sometimes with bullfrogs sitting on them. These didn't have flowers, and the pads didn't look big enough to hold a frog.

She looked at him, to see if he was making it up.

But he was already off the bridge and heading down the bank. "I'll get you some," he said.

He was all the way down by the water before she

found her voice. "I can't use them," she said. "I need another tree leaf."

"Just the same," he answered. He bent over, disappearing into the weeds. She heard him splash through the water as he pulled at the leaves. "These bastards are tough," he called to her.

Finally he straightened up and raised the plant to show her: a soggy green weed that had nothing to do with anything.

He stood smiling at her from the creek, holding the plant high in the air. The grass grew to his waist, and he looked small, like a boy, and far away.

"This is really something," he called to her. "Isn't this something?"

Josie felt funny inside, empty. It reminded her of the day her mother had moved all of Josie's father's things out of his office at home, and the room echoed and felt so strange. Now she wondered if Uncle Jo Jo would have to go live in a rented room, too, like her father. She wondered if Cousin Eddie would ever come back, and if she'd even be there when he did.

"It's a weed," she told Uncle Jo Jo. Her voice sounded odd to her, like it wasn't even her own.

Jo Jo dropped his arm and looked at her. "You mean you don't want it?" he asked.

She wished she never had to see any of them again. She shook her head. "No," she told Jo Jo.

They headed for the car, and the gravel crunched under their feet. "Well, you couldn't have asked for a more beautiful day," Jo Jo sighed. He sounded pretty sad about it.

Just as they reached the car Jo Jo turned to her. "Everything's okay," he said. "Right, little pardner?" He moved his head, searching, like he was trying to find something in her eyes. And then he found what he was looking for and held on.

"Okay," she said, and she got in the car.

But before he could start the engine she had left without him, going someplace she shouldn't be.

DIFFICULT PASSAGE

We never spoke of the canal as anything very important. We never said, "It is because of the canal that we are here." At most we would say, "The canal is high today." Or, "The canal is low today." "It's covered with scum." "It stinks in this weather."

That summer when we wheeled Ole Papa to the bridge he let out a scream that stopped us cold. He was eighty-two and by that time both legs had been amputated. We had meant to wheel him over the bridge for a look at the new housing project when he cried out and we stopped. We looked up and down the still water. It was one of those hot days when the only sound is the whine of the cicadas up in the trees. The water was low and covered with scum, and I felt that I was just beginning to understand something, although I did not have a name for it.

Ole Papa's father had moved here from a little town on the Adriatic because he had heard that a man could get rich in America working on the canal. He came, and he worked, but he didn't get rich. Eventually his son, our Ole Papa, started working the water, too, loading the barges with onions and potatoes to send down to the cities. That was when Ole Papa was fifteen, the same year he met our grandmother.

The two of them, and then later their children, swam in that water in the summer and skated on it in the winter. They stood on the lift bridge as it was raised and lowered and watched the boats that came from New York and Albany loaded with spools of wire or bales of linen or furniture or tins of food or tobacco. And Ole Papa pulled his first son, the brother our father was named after, out of that water one March day when the ice was thin and it was already too late to save him.

You had to cross the canal to get to the cemetery. After they took you from Lou Grasso's parlor and had the mass said for you at church, your last ride carried you over the canal. Ole Papa had followed many friends and family members on their last ride, and most recently it was his wife who had made the trip. So that day, when he cried out as we tried to wheel him across, we had the good sense to turn around and take him back home.

I loved Ole Papa fiercely, and claimed him as my own. I took delight in wheeling him around town, spoon-feeding him, because he couldn't feed himself (nor could he "talk" in anything more than a grunt), adjusting his clothes, patting his bald head, and talking to him in the way I might have talked to a favorite doll or a younger sister. Ordinarily my parents thought of me as stubborn, wild, a little too imaginative for my own good, embarrassingly and hopelessly tomboyish. But they took solace in the fact that I was mature, responsible, and even somewhat maternal when it came to Ole Papa. They never had to ask me to watch him. I did it on my own because he was mine.

Father was always away working. When he wasn't at the factory rebuilding transmissions for school buses, he was out on Uncle Paul's farm, helping him top or weed or screen onions. Mother was often sick with her headaches, and couldn't take care of Ole Papa. After her operation, the one she had when the baby wouldn't come right, her headaches started. Sometimes they'd last a week. We'd all have to clear out of the house then, and she'd lie in bed with the shades down and a wet washcloth on her forehead until Father came home. Then he'd fry potatoes and eggs for our supper, and he'd open a can of pears for her because that was the only thing she could eat when she had her headaches, canned pears. If we had to ask her something she'd put her hand to her head and say, "Shh. *Whisper* to me," and we would whisper.

It was later that same summer, in mid-August, that I took Ole Papa to the canal bridge a second time and wheeled him over the bridge, deaf to his protests. The circus had come to town. Teddy and I had been to church socials, and we had been to the county fair, but we had never been to a circus. I had saved a dollar and a quarter; Teddy had eighty-five cents. We couldn't count on Father taking us, even though he had said, "Maybe," because after work he had to help Uncle Paul. And two days before the circus came Mother's headaches came too. But I knew I would steal, I would lie, I would do anything to get there.

We had seen the posters around town, and we had talked to some of our friends, imagining, and then elaborating on our imagination of what it would be like. Mostly, though, Teddy and I talked to each other of the wonders we would see, of the exotic animals, elephants and camels. In the dark of the night, in quiet voices, we talked of the freaks we'd seen in the advertisements, especially the man made of India rubber. He could twist his body into any number of unnatural positions, and make horrid, grotesque faces. Teddy thought it was because he was born with no bones, and we debated the idea for a while until we realized that most likely he would not be able to stand up if he had no bones. At any rate, there was something frighteningly wrong with the man. We had to see him.

The posters also promised the Amazing and Mysterious Zonzono, Master of Levitation and Other Dark Secrets That Will Astonish and Amaze You. I had recently been reading about magic and the powers of the mind, and Teddy and I had been practicing magic on each other. We'd read each other's minds, concentrating with a passion that forced the other's nose to itch, hypnotizing each other and convincing ourselves that our arms *did* grow heavy, we really *couldn't* move them if we tried, and we *were* in a deep trance. And during those days, whenever I wheeled Ole Papa anywhere, in my heart of hearts I pretended I was one of the men who set up the circus and I was wheeling the legless wonder to the sideshow tent. Even then I was horrified at my thoughts, and didn't speak a word of them to anyone, not even to Teddy.

On the day of the circus, Teddy looked at me, forlorn. He had his eighty-five cents tied up in an old sock that he had wrapped around his wrist. We were on the porch. Mother was lying in bed with the shades down, and Father was at work. Ole Papa sat on the porch with us, tilted to one side in his wheelchair, his head flopped over, snoring. "What are we going to do?" Teddy said. Earlier I had thought of just leaving Ole Papa while we took off. But if Mother got up, if Father came home, or, heaven forbid, if Aunt Ruby stopped by to see that everything was all right, we would be in for the belt. But I really didn't want to leave Ole Papa because he needed watching. Sometimes he got thirsty or hungry or lonely or scared. And sometimes he got himself all slouched over in that chair and needed to be hoisted up and straightened around. "We're taking him with us," I told Teddy. Then I knelt down in front of Ole Papa, and put my hands on his hands, and shook him.

"Poppi, Poppi, you want to go to the circus?" He lifted his head and looked around. "Me and Teddy's going to the circus," I told him. Then he saw me and stared. "You want to go for a walk, Poppi? You want to go see some elephants and camels?"

He grunted out, "Huh." It was the one word he used for both "yes" and "no."

"I think he said no," Teddy said.

"You dope," I told him. "Take him to the bathroom and give him his pee can while I get my money."

He looked at me.

"Go on," I told him.

Teddy maneuvered Ole Papa through the doorway while I ran upstairs for my own sock full of money that I'd hidden in the heat register. When I passed Mother's door she whispered my name, so I went in. She held the washcloth out to me. "Will you wet it," she said. "Cold." I ran the faucet a long time and came back with the wet washcloth. She folded it across her forehead.

"We're taking Ole Papa for a walk," I told her.

"Shhh," she said. "Keep him out of the sun."

"We will," I whispered, and I tiptoed out.

Teddy was trying to get Ole Papa back through the door onto the porch. "Did he do anything?" I asked. I held the door for him.

"Some," he said.

"I told Mama we're going for a walk." We wheeled down the ramp and out to the sidewalk. I jostled Ole Papa on the shoulder. "I bet you never saw a circus *or* a camel, did you, Poppi?" He made no answer, and I took over pushing the wheelchair.

Teddy and I talked about how much money it was all going to cost. It would be fifty cents to get in, that much we knew, but we didn't know if they'd charge for seeing things once you were inside. All I really cared about was the sideshow, but to Teddy everything was a wonder, and he wanted to see it all. We decided we'd better hold on to our change until we found out how much everything cost. We weren't going to miss the India Rubber Man, and I knew as well that no matter what I was going to see the Amazing and Mysterious Zonzono do his levitation act.

The circus was set up out in the vacant lot near the old canning factory, not quite a mile from our house. There was sidewalk for most of the way, at least until you got right to the factory. Then you had to walk in the road. The only hard part about getting there was going to be crossing the canal bridge with Ole Papa. As we got closer to the bridge, Teddy and I started talking faster and louder, and then I started firing questions at Ole Papa about the kinds of strange animals he'd seen in his time, and about

India Rubber Men—had he ever seen one and did he know where they came from and what made them that way?

When we got to the bridge Ole Papa started grunting out, "Huh, huh," and we knew that those "huh's" meant "no." We stopped. Somebody was walking across on the other side, and he watched us as he walked past. We waited until Ole Papa was quiet, but his hands gripped the armrests. I knew he was mad. But there wasn't anything else to do. I nodded at Teddy, and we hightailed it over the bridge, pushing the wheelchair while Ole Papa let out a bloodcurdling scream. We didn't stop once we reached the other side. I kept running down the sidewalk until we were almost to Coleman's store and then I realized people were looking at us, so I slowed down. Ole Papa was making huffing noises and hitting the armrest. Teddy's face was the color of chalk. "We're gonna get in trouble," he said, and I knew he was right. But we were across the bridge, and there was no turning back.

We strained to catch sight of the circus, but the canning factory blocked our view. Still, you could smell it, a smell that is unlike anything else in the world. When the sidewalk ended I wheeled Ole Papa into the road and we walked in silence, looking ahead. Then we passed the factory and there it was, looming before us like a vision: the one giant tent with three peaks, and a smaller tent, and trucks, and bales of hay, and people in costumes, small wooden stalls with clusters of people standing around, music, everything, all hitting you at once.

"We're here, Poppi," I told him. He sat gripping the armrest, his head held rigid, and I knew he was mad. Teddy stood with his mouth open, taking everything in. Then he started unwinding the sock wound around his wrist, and we headed for the entrance.

The man was saying, "Step right up, folks," just like he was supposed to say. But he didn't look like he was supposed to look. He was a kid, not much older than me, with stringy hair and a faded T-shirt. Teddy gave him fifty cents and got his ticket. I plunked my two quarters down and stared at him as he ripped a ticket off. Then I went through.

"Whoa there," he called. "Hey you, girl."

I turned around.

"What about the old man?" he said. "Fifty cents for the old man."

I could feel my face go red. I went back and gave him two more quarters, and didn't even think to make Teddy split it with me. Teddy just shook his head when I went back in. Then he shrugged.

What struck me about the people inside was how odd they all looked, not just the circus people, but everybody. They weren't the sort of crowd you'd see in church on Sunday, or even what you'd see at the train station or in the grocery store Friday nights. They were the circus crowd, and we were part of it.

We didn't go in the main tent, even though that's where most of the other people were headed. Instead we walked down to the concession stands and looked around. Besides the popcorn and candied-apple booths, there were all kinds of games, a dozen or so in a row, with a man or woman shouting at us to buy something, try something, win something, only a nickel or a dime. Teddy wanted to stop and smash plates so he could win a pirate bank, but I told him to wait a bit, till we'd checked the whole place out. Ole Papa sat wide-eyed. He didn't grunt, and he didn't pound the armrests. He just looked.

At the end of the row of stalls was the smaller tent. A

rope hung across the entrance, and on it a sign saying Twenty-five Cents. You could hear noise inside, music, and words like *amazing, incredible,* and *right before your eyes* drifting out. We looked at the posters propped against the canvas. One showed a man with snakes wound around his neck and arms and stomach. Another had a fat lady in a flowered dress sitting in a tiny chair. On another a man wearing a cape was sawing a lady in two, and on another a tall man had his legs crossed twice, it seemed, and his arms twisted around his neck as if he were trying to put his right elbow in his left ear.

"It's him," I told Teddy.

"Is it him?" he said. We stared. "Crimast," he said after a while. His own arm went up around his neck as he looked at the poster.

"Come on," I told him.

"We going in now?"

"No, dope, not now. We have to wait for the next show."

We wheeled back down into the big tent. The bleachers were half-full, and music was playing. A man with a long stick was taking a bow and next to him an enormous elephant bowed too. They walked out while people clapped, the elephant rocking from side to side and stepping slow like he was too old and tired to lift those heavy feet. Men rushed around, moving boxes and tightening wires. We parked Ole Papa in the front row. The seats were full down there, so we squatted in the dirt next to him.

"You having fun, Poppi?" I asked. It was the first time since we'd left home that I'd taken a good look at him. He was beginning to slouch over in the chair, so we pulled him up. He grunted, "Huh, huh," when we touched him, and once we got him straightened up he glared at me, furious. "We're at the circus, Poppi," I told him. "It's going to be fun." Music sounded over the loudspeaker, and the men who had been working in the center ring hurried out. "Look there," I said to Ole Papa, and I pointed to the ring. He continued to glare at me. I had a sudden thought that there was something terribly wrong with our being there, and I wanted to rush out with Ole Papa and Teddy and go back home. But somebody near us said, "Here they come," and I looked up to see a family of acrobats tumbling into the arena. They built a human pyramid with a girl who was younger than Teddy and dressed in a silver bathing suit standing on the very top of the pyramid. Then the man and woman got on opposite ends of the tightrope and walked toward each other while their kids did stunts on the ground. They didn't have a net, but they didn't need one. The tightrope was only about six feet high.

Next came the clowns, a fat one that kept falling into a barrel and a skinny one that kept trying to keep the fat one out. A lion tamer entered a cage that had been set up inside the arena. The lions paced, their roars like loud yawns. A midget rode a unicycle and threw bubble gum at us. Then there was exotic music and a woman dressed in silky handkerchiefs, with one handkerchief covering her face, rode out on a camel. Teddy squatted with his hands on his knees, craning his head forward to see, his face flushed with the wonder of it all. But all I could think about was how long it would be before the sideshow started.

The camel had one hump and, like the elephant, seemed old and tired.

"It looks like a horse," I told Teddy. I looked over at Ole Papa. He was watching the arena, but I don't know what he was seeing or what he was thinking, or if he was

thinking anything. When I noticed the tufts of hair growing from his ears, a deep sadness came over me.

"Let's go," I told Teddy. The dancing ponies were
just coming out and he wanted to stay. "I'm going," I told
him. I stood up and started pushing Ole Papa toward the
door and Teddy followed. He kept looking behind us,
though, as the ponies danced in a circle while a lady rode
standing up on one pony's back. "We can come back
later," I told him, but I knew we wouldn't.

We headed for the sideshow. I caught sight of Old
Man Stanford from the diner, watching some kids throw
darts at balloons. It looked like he was there alone, without
his wife or grandchildren. Just as we passed him he turned
his head and saw us, but we kept going. I told Teddy he
could try for that pirate bank on the way out, after we'd
seen the India Rubber Man.

I was beginning to worry about Ole Papa. It was a hot
day, and I thought he must be getting thirsty. I was thirsty.
But I was afraid to give him anything to drink because then
he'd have to go to the bathroom and we'd really be in
trouble. If he didn't have his can he just went in his pants.
"You okay, Poppi?" I asked him. He didn't say anything.

We had to wait outside the tent for the next show to
begin, so we looked again at the pictures of the freaks. I
remembered my daydream of pushing the legless man up
onstage for the show. "We better leave Ole Papa out here,"
I told Teddy.

"Why?"

"We just better. He can't go in there."

"He'll fit," Teddy said. "Look at how wide it is."

"Never mind. I'm going to park him under this tree.
You think he'll be all right?"

"I don't know if we should leave him," he said.

I knew we shouldn't leave him, but I also knew that we shouldn't take him in. And I knew, too, that no matter what, I was going in.

"You stay with him," I told Teddy.

"Are you nuts?" he said.

So we put Ole Papa's brakes on under the tree, and we hoisted him up in his chair, and I patted him and told him not to worry, that we'd be right back. He scowled at me with a look of absolute hatred. We paid our money and went in. I didn't look back at the old man. I was afraid to.

You could only go one way in the tent because they had the inside roped off and partitioned into a line of rooms. Each room held one of the spectacles. The fat lady was fat, but not much fatter than Old Lady Bass who lived behind the beauty shop downtown. She sat in her chair and let you look at her while a midget told you how old she was and how much she weighed and what she ate every day.

The snake charmer came closest to impressing us. The enormous snakes, unlike anything we'd seen, wound around his body. They slithered and arched and raised their heads and looked at you with their snake eyes while they flicked their tongues. I saw Teddy shiver when the snake coiled around the man's face, and I shivered, too.

I don't know what we were expecting to see in the India Rubber Man. Maybe we thought he wouldn't be human after all or that if he was human he wouldn't have bones, just like Teddy had said. But he looked pretty much like anyone else, except for being a little too tall and a little too thin, and maybe a little on the grotesque side which, I was beginning to realize, was the way most people looked. His face was a rough one, covered with bumps and gouges, a face that might have been punched a few times. He went through his stretches. "Buddy Pellnick can do that," Teddy said. The man twisted his arm around his neck, crossed his legs double, lay down on the floor, and said he was going to make a human knot. It didn't look like a knot. It looked like one of the exercises they make the first graders do in gym because they don't know how to do anything else. Somebody next to me said the man was double-jointed. "I bet Buddy can do that, too," Teddy said. All that time I thought the India Rubber Man was leading up to something big—that he would twist into some impossible, inhuman form. But he stood up, said thank-you, bowed, and went out the back of his room. At first Teddy looked surprised. Then he looked disgusted. We walked on to the next room.

"You want to go now?" he asked me.

"Don't you want to see Zonzono?" I asked him.

"I don't know," he said. He kicked at some straw on the ground.

"You go wait with Ole Papa," I told him. "I'll be right out."

He kept kicking at the straw, but he didn't leave.

Zonzono entered in a whirlwind of crashing cymbals, his cape flying, his beard and mustache jet black. He spoke with a deep voice so that, even from the start, it seemed you were being hypnotized. He did a few card tricks, then one with boxes and a walnut, and one with a pitcher of water that he poured into a napkin and then back from the napkin into the pitcher. He guessed somebody's name and somebody else's birthday, and he made a boy disappear in a trunk and made him come back. I was half-trying to figure out the catch to each trick because I was afraid that underneath it all he, too, might be a fake. Yet I believed, or wanted to believe, and when he called for another volunteer my hand was in the air before I knew what I was volunteering for. I strained my arm and waved my hand, looking at him beseechingly. Perhaps I had powers, too, because he pointed at me and said, "Yes, you."

I climbed the three steps to his stage in a delirium. I had left my brother without a second thought. I had left the audience and was oblivious to their presence. I felt no fear or doubt or shame. All I knew was that I was standing next to the amazing and mysterious Zonzono, who had chosen me out of all the others, and who was now whispering in my ear on the sly as he talked to the audience in his deep, magnificent voice. To them he described his gravity-defying levitation act. To me he whispered, "Lie down on the platform, keep your eyes shut, and don't move until I tell you." He pushed me gently back onto the platform while he told the audience how I was going into a deep trance. "Close your eyes," he told me.

There is something disorienting about lying on your back on a metal table in a tent in front of dozens of strangers, your eyes closed, your ears attuned to the sounds of the crowd. I was drifting, drifting. A thin blanket was placed over me. There was silence, and then I was drifting some more. I became terrified. I turned my head in what seemed to be darkness. I opened my eyes a bit more and thought I saw a horizontal bar connected to the platform on which I lay. It crossed my mind that such a bar might serve to raise and lower the platform.

I was afraid everyone had left. I wondered if Zonzono had told me to get up or if he had gone, too. I raised my shoulders and he pushed me back and told me to keep still. He was telling the audience how he was passing a hoop over and around my body that was suspended in midair to prove there were no gimmicks or devices involved. A whoosh of air passed over me. Then I was being lowered and Zonzono told me to come out of my trance. I got up, blinking. He helped me off the platform, and I walked back to my brother, dizzy and confused.

I was vaguely aware of people around me, of their voices and their movements, but that was all. Minutes passed. Slowly, I became conscious of Zonzono onstage, finishing up one of his tricks, then thanking us all, sweeping his cape around to the sound of clashing cymbals and applause.

We walked out. Teddy hung close to me. After a while I asked him, "Did you see it?"

"I saw," he said, nodding.

"Was I in the air?"

"Yeah." He looked dazed. "Were you hypnotized?" he asked.

"I don't know," I said. "I don't know what happened. What happened?" I asked him.

And then he told me all about the hoop and how I was floating in the air. "Crimast, it was spooky," he said.

When we reached Ole Papa I was surprised at how different he looked, like something had happened to him while we were gone. His face seemed sad and lost, and he looked past us to the trees beyond the tents. Even when we spoke to him his face didn't change. Old Man Stanford from the diner was lurking near him, watching while we straightened Ole Papa up. "Where's your mother and father?" he asked us.

"They're not here," we told him. He watched us undo the brake.

"Are you kids here alone?" We didn't answer him. "Do your parents know where you took your grandpa?"

"We take Ole Papa anywhere," I told him, and I started wheeling away fast, afraid he'd think I was being smart.

"I wonder what your father is going to say about all this," Stanford said.

"Cripes Almighty," I said to Teddy when we'd gone a distance. We didn't say anything else, either one of us, we just went, and fast.

When we got to the sidewalk Teddy wondered if it was past suppertime. "It's not that late," I told him. But I wasn't sure.

"We're going to get it," he said.

"I know it," I said. "I know it. You don't have to keep reminding me."

If there is such a thing as true remorse for your sins, then that is what I felt as I wheeled Ole Papa home. On the way to the circus, and even while sitting under the big top, I had had my moments of doubt and my twinges of guilt. But now I feared that something irrevocable had taken place. I had betrayed my grandfather. As we trudged along in silence, I imagined all I would do to try to make things right between Ole Papa and me: I would sneak him a piece of chocolate, which he wasn't supposed to eat, or I would help him hold the neighbor's dog, because he loved dogs and ours died last year, or I would find the money to buy a pint of strawberry ice cream, his favorite, and feed it to him in secret.

We got to the bridge, and I took a deep breath. I could see Teddy brace himself, but we were too exhausted or bewildered to even bother trying to divert Ole Papa's attention this time. All I said was "We're almost home, Poppi." I tightened my grip and pushed, not running, but moving fast just the same. Ole Papa sat there holding the armrests, and he didn't make a sound. His pale head bobbed along as we hit the cracks in the walk. Then we were over, and none of us said a word, we just kept going.

It was Ole Papa's silence that finally got to me. When we reached home I wheeled him into the kitchen. Mother was still in bed and Father hadn't come in from work. I pushed Ole Papa up to the table and poured him a glass of water, then peeled a banana and put it down on the table near him. A banana was about the only thing he could eat without help. Teddy slipped away without a word, going up to his room, I supposed. I felt that I should touch Ole Papa, or hold him, or say something to him, but I couldn't do any of those things. I waited for him to look at me. He kept his eyes on the glass of water. There was no expression in his face—nothing, nothing at all. I ran out the back door.

I climbed the pear tree and sat there waiting. I could feel something welling inside me. But I felt dried up, too, and beyond tears. I didn't know what was going to happen when Father found out, and I knew he would find out because either I would tell him, or Old Man Stanford would, or else we both would.

I started thinking about the strange and solitary man I could not know, my grandfather. And I thought, too, about all of us, about my grandmother who was dead, and my father and his dead brother whose name he had, about my mother and her lost baby and her headaches, me and Teddy, all of us.

I touched the bark of the pear tree. I had been transformed and levitated, suspended in midair so that a hoop passed over and around my body proved beyond the shadow of a doubt that no trickery was involved. I had seen some of the wonders the world had to offer.

Yet everything, everything felt old.

A
PLACE
OF
LIGHT

When Robert's car broke down the second time, he said, "You kids stay out of my hair. Go across that ditch to those weeds." Ma leaned her head against the window and looked out. She wasn't crying. "You, Injun," he said to me. "Take the blanket and get." Naomi followed me through the tall weeds. We could hear him swearing back there. Already we were getting bit up. We peed, then we spread the blanket and sat down.

We heard him swear and bang on the car, and Ma told him to go find help, there was nothing else he could do by himself. Naomi lay down on her side, her back to me. I thought about the way she slept in the night lately, with her fists clenched and her eyes squeezed shut. I said her name, but she didn't answer. She was the oldest and had always been the boss. You'd never know it now.

I think Naomi stopped talking somewhere in West Virginia, when she realized we weren't going back. Now we were across the border into Alabama. Heading for Galveston, Robert said. She hated him, maybe more than I did.

It was okay the year he went away. Ma didn't even mention his name. She took his picture off her dresser and laid it facedown in the drawer, under her stockings. Then he came back, just like that, and the picture went up again. He started right in with his fighting.

"Why'd you let him come back?" I asked Ma.

"I don't know" was all she said.

"If he hits me once—" I told her.

She looked down at her hands. "He's not going to hit you," she said.

"Or you," I said.

She shook her head, still looking down at her hands.

Once, I heard her say she used to love him. "He was so good to me after their daddy died," she said. She was talking to our neighbor, though, not to me.

I remember when Robert came to live with us, after our father died. I remember, too, the story Ma would tell about when I was born, how I looked so dark—red-skinned and with lots of black hair—that she thought they had given her the wrong baby. "She looked just like an Indian," she said. Robert heard that story, and he started calling me Injun and saying how someday he would find an Indian family to send me back to, where I belonged. Ma heard him talk like that to me, but never said a word, so I wondered if it was true that I was the wrong baby.

When things got really bad with Robert, though, Ma said what she felt like to him. Sometimes he'd slap her for it, sometimes he didn't do anything. You never knew when it was coming. He'd gone after us just once and Ma lit into him, fists and all. Then afterward, because we were scared and crying, she came into our room. She stood in the doorway, like a caught animal. She held on to the doorframe with both hands. "It's all right," she told us from where she stood. "You'll be all right," she said. She didn't come any closer.

Now Robert was going to Galveston to work because he knew somebody there. Really he was going to get away from "trouble"—all the people he owed money to. "Mean son of a bitches," he called them. "Just love to kick a man when he's down." He made Ma buy the car with the fifty dollars he gave her, and he put some old plates on it that he found somewhere. Ma wanted to get to Galveston as much as he did. She had a cousin who lived nearby in Beaumont, and an aunt, too, and maybe they could help us. She didn't tell Robert about the cousin and the aunt.

"You thirsty?" I said to Naomi.

"Uh-uh."

Something skittered through the grass, and I jumped, held still, listened. I heard more sounds: bugs, birds, animals, the breeze through the grass. The afternoon sun beat down. A nearby tree gave some shade. I lay down, too. I rolled over so I was touching Naomi, and I fell asleep.

I woke to the sounds of Robert banging on the car, still trying to fix it. Naomi shaded her eyes with her hand and watched a gray bird in the tree.

Ma called, "Audrey. Naomi. Where are you?"

We went back to the car. Ma was sitting in front, on the passenger side, with the door open. She was combing her hair. Her face was flushed from the heat. She started pinning up her hair, and it made her face look thin and old.

Robert leaned under the hood. Tools lay on the fender. "You go in those woods," he told me. "I saw some kind of shack in there. Maybe somebody lives there." He pointed. He knew better than to tell Naomi to do anything. She wouldn't look at him or answer him. Once, when Ma wasn't around, he slapped her face for it. She didn't even blink.

"You tell 'em the car's broke down," Robert said. "Tell 'em come help."

I looked at Ma. "Go ahead," she told me. "We're not going anywhere." She knew I was thinking about that time he drove me and Naomi out in the country and made me get out because he said I was acting smart. He came back and got me half an hour later.

I was just turning to go when an old pickup truck came down the road. It was the only traffic since we'd stopped. We had to take what Robert called the back roads because he was afraid of being pulled over. Robert stood on the shoulder to flag them down. It was hot out. The hair around his ears and against his neck was wet. The truck slowed and they stared at us as they went by, an old man and old lady. She had a polka dot kerchief tied around her head. A big yellow dog in the back of the truck barked at us as they went by.

"Son of a bitching bastards," Robert said. He kicked at an empty cigarette wrapper on the side of the road, and the dust blew back against his pant leg. "Go on," he told me.

I didn't see any house, but I headed where he'd pointed.

"And see if they got anything to eat," he called after me.

The woods were full of tiny bugs. I slapped at them as they went for my face and arms. I kept looking back. The blue of the car showed through the trees. Then the trees closed and I didn't see the car anymore. I went back a few steps until I could see it again, to make sure they hadn't left. I looked ahead through the woods, trying to make out a house. I wondered if Robert had been lying. I started walking again, but I didn't know if I was going in the right direction. Then I parted some branches so I could pass on, and I stepped into a new place.

It was an open place, full of light. The grass was short, growing right down close with the earth. Stones and small boulders cropped out from the wide, rolling field. A few clumps of tall weeds with bright purple and yellow flowers stood out against the pale grass and the white rocks. Farther out was a run-down house, and next to it a shed of the same weathered boards. One tree shaded the house, and under the tree was a rusted barrel with red chickens strutting around it.

After a minute, I noticed the cow, on the very edge of the open place, in a little patch of shade from the woods, not far from where I stood. The cow watched me, its big eyes blinking. It was a ghost cow, the color of bone. I held still and waited. Then I moved my arms and took a few steps to see if the cow would charge. It kept chewing and watching. I headed for the house. The cow followed, slow, keeping its distance.

I reached the back of the house, then had to walk past the chickens to get to the front. The cow stayed behind with the chickens, nosing around the barrel with them.

A long open porch ran the length of the house, and two rickety steps led up to the porch. A black girl in a print dress sat at the top of the steps, her knees apart, her legs reaching down to the bottom step. She wore red high-top sneakers. Her braids were coming undone, and she had bits of dried grass in her hair. In the dip of her skirt she held an aluminum bowl half-filled with green beans. On the porch beside her lay a newspaper heaped with the beans. She stopped in the middle of snapping them.

"What you want?" she asked.

She was blacker than anyone I'd ever seen, and shiny, just like she'd been oiled and polished. She looked about Naomi's age, but her breasts were bigger. The blouse pulled tight across her breasts, flattening them. Her face was wide, with a big nose and mouth, and she looked like she could hurt somebody.

"You a dummy?" she said. "Can't you talk?"

"Our car broke down," I told her.

"So?" She snapped the beans and flicked the ends into the flower bed alongside the porch.

"Can somebody help us?"

She eyed me up and down. "You come to a sorry place for help," she told me. "Mama," she said.

From somewhere on the porch, a woman's voice said, "Whose child is this?"

I looked up at the shadow inside the screen door. The girl flicked the bean ends.

"Says their car's broke down." The girl spoke without turning.

"Nobody'll stop," I told the shadow. "We been waiting all afternoon."

"Ain't that a shame," the girl said, snapping the beans.

The woman asked, "And who is 'we'?"

"Me, my sister, and my mother. And my mother's husband."

The girl snorted.

"Well," the woman said. She opened the screen door and stepped out. "Well, well." She was tall and big and full of muscles. Her hair was cut short and was sprinkled with gray. She wore a flower print dress like the girl's, only not as faded. She, too, wore sneakers, but hers were cut low and were the color of dirt.

"You'll find a garage five miles in to town," she said.

"Can I use your telephone?" I asked.

The girl laughed.

The woman said, "Gilberts is the only ones with a telephone. Town's closer."

Robert had told me to find the house and ask for help, that's all. I decided to go back to the car and let him find the garage himself.

"Hyacinth," the woman said. "Take this child to her car and see what you can see."

"Probably out of gas and don't know it," the girl said. She plunked the aluminum bowl down on the porch and looked at me. "Ain't that about right?" The girl stood and stretched. She was tall and big-boned like the woman. She worked her mouth, like she was chewing, then spit a glob of brown drool into the dirt near me. Her eyes narrowed, as if she would smile.

"When the angel blows his trumpet," the woman said to her, "I pray the Lord will be kind enough to let you hear."

"I bet you ain't got no tools, either," the girl said to me.

"We got some," I told her.

"Huh," she said.

"Take Samuel and drag that car back here if you worried about tools," the woman told her. "At least you be off the road and where it's cooler."

The girl walked away and called into the air, making a sound like a squirrel. She went into the shed. The woman looked up at the sky. "Keep burning my back," she said. She picked up the bowl and went inside.

The girl came out with a harness folded over one shoulder. "You coming or ain't you?" she said.

I started back the way I'd come.

"If it's all right with you," she said, "I'll be taking the road." She headed down the driveway. A thin mule stepped from behind the shed and plodded along with her. The cow followed the mule, nosing its tail. The girl looked back at me and shook her head. "If you waiting for the Kingdom coming, you got a long wait."

I followed the girl, the mule, and the cow. At the end of the driveway we turned right, onto the road. The cow stayed behind, dropping its heavy head into a clump of grass. There were woods on both sides, and then up ahead I saw the car, and Robert and my mother.

Robert came out to meet us. When he saw it was me, he said, "What the Jesus hell?"

The girl dropped the harness. She glanced at Ma and Naomi. "Your car got gas?" she asked Robert.

"Course it does. Damn fuel pump's gone," he said. "Did you find somebody to help us?" Robert asked me.

"Maybe she did," the girl said. She was already in front of the car, looking under the hood. The mule nibbled leaves from a bush. Ma stood beside the car, her hands folded against her stomach, watching Hyacinth. Naomi sat on the grass in the shade. Her eyes, too, were on the black girl.

"Is somebody coming?" Robert said to me. Hyacinth got in the car and tried to start it. When Robert heard the engine turn over he took a step forward and called, "Hey. What do you think you're doing?" She kept cranking the engine, but it only sputtered.

"You. Get out of there," Robert told her. He reached in to pull her out.

"Thanks, but I don't need no help," she said. She stood up.

"Just what do you think you're doing?"

The girl walked to the front of the car and took up a screwdriver. "Is this all the tools you got?" She began poking under the hood.

Naomi stood up in her spot of shade, and Ma stepped closer to the car, her hands still folded in front of her, the fingers fidgeting. Robert grabbed the screwdriver from the girl.

She straightened up. "That ain't no busted fuel pump you got, neither," she said.

"What do you know?" Robert said.

"I know you going nowheres in this car," she told him. She nodded her head at the car, but she kept her eyes on Robert.

I saw that look come into Robert's face. "She came to help us," I told him.

"There's no help she can give me," he said.

The girl said nothing. She stood working her mouth, then let sail a glob of brown tobacco spit past Robert's leg. It landed with a splat behind him.

Robert didn't say anything for a minute. Then he started gathering his tools from the fender, moving his arms more than he had to. Ma and the black girl's eyes met while Robert collected his things. Ma seemed ready to say something to her.

Robert said, "You want to help, get us a tow truck."

"That's just what I done," she said. "I don't plan to spend the day passing between home and here toting wrenches." The girl picked up the harness she'd dropped and carried it to the mule. Naomi held a handful of grass out to the animal. It nibbled from her hand.

"I'm going to ask your old bones to do a little work, Samuel. There now," the girl said to the mule. She rubbed the top of its head, between the ears. She led the mule to the car and attached the ends of the harness underneath the front of the car.

"You wait a minute," Robert said.

"You won't find no other help on this road, mister," the girl told him. "Take it or leave it."

Robert didn't answer.

The girl led the mule forward a few steps and looked behind at the straps as they pulled taut.

"Can you steer this car?" she said to me. I nodded yes. "Then get in behind the wheel," she said. "I don't want Samuel taking no more load than he's got to." She looked at Robert when she said this.

I got in, and she walked the mule back onto the road. I steered the car behind the animal, and Hyacinth took us back the way we'd come. She was a big girl, but when she walked, the dirt beneath her feet didn't stir.

"You hauling this car to a garage?" Robert asked. He and Ma and Naomi followed alongside the car, off the road.

"I sure ain't," the girl said.

We stopped in front of the house. Robert played with the pack of cigarettes in his shirt pocket. Ma looked around

at the house and field and flower garden. Hyacinth un-
hitched the mule.

"You got anybody here can fix this car?" Robert said.

The woman came out and stood on the porch. She and
Ma nodded hello to each other, then Ma looked away.
"There's water there if you're thirsty," the woman said.
She pointed to the pump. "What is it?" she asked her
daughter.

"Maybe needs a new coil," Hyacinth told her. Then
to herself she said, "We'll see about getting into town."

"Can't your mule tow us in?" Robert asked.

"He don't go that far pulling a load," the girl said.
"Bad leg."

The woman nodded at the girl, then she turned to go
back in the house. "You're welcome inside where it's
cooler," she told us. "I got work to do."

The girl carried the harness into the shed. The mule
laid back its ears and blew air from its lips. The white cow
trotted over from behind the house, as if it had been called,
and the two animals rubbed noses. Robert squatted on his
heels and lit a cigarette. "Good God Almighty," he said.

Hyacinth came back with her tools and lifted the car's
hood. "We got to be sure of this," she said. She tried the
engine again and listened. Robert squatted and smoked his
cigarette, watching her.

"The girl says it's five miles to town," he said to her.

"That's right."

"How late's that garage open?"

"Late," Hyacinth told him. "Till dark."

Robert watched her, thinking. "You got a car?" he
asked.

"No sir." She kept working under the hood.

"Truck? Tractor?"

"I got a bicycle, but it's got a flat tire. And one of the pedals is missing. Maybe I can get into town for you a little bye and bye. 'Less you want to go." She looked at him. "Awful hot on foot now."

Robert ran his hand through his hair. He looked around. "What about that mule? Can I ride that mule to town?"

Hyacinth stopped and looked at him a minute. "I sure don't think you can," she said. She stuck her head under the hood. "Anyways, he's a working mule, not a riding mule."

"Well, Christ," Robert said. He looked at Hyacinth as she bent under the hood. He shook his head, slow.

The pump clanged and squeaked as Ma worked it. There was a tin pail under the spout and a tin cup tied by a string to the pipe. She called, "Audrey, Naomi, come have a drink." Naomi turned when Ma said her name. Her hand was stretched out, her fingers touching the cow's face.

"It's nice and cool," Ma said. She sipped from the tin cup, then smiled. We went over and drank with her.

Then Ma said, "Robert, I am going in the house."

"What you going in there for?"

"It's too hot out here. And I have been invited," she said. "Are you girls coming?" Naomi went back to the animals without answering. I shook my head no. I was hot, but I wanted to watch the black girl.

"If you know what's good for you," Robert told her, "you better not go in there."

Ma started for the house. Naomi stood near the animals, watching.

"That's right. You go ahead, then," Robert told her. "Just remember, you got to come back out. And I'll be right here when you do."

Hyacinth straightened up. Her face was dark and serious, and she looked hard at Robert. I could see him get worried. She said, "I'm taking this bad coil outta your car. I hope you got some money. You going to need it."

Robert stood and watched Ma climb the two steps to the porch. She knocked, then opened the door and went inside. Robert threw the cigarette in the dirt. He shoved his hands into his pockets and turned, looking across the planted fields.

Naomi watched him, her hands at her sides, closed.

I stood next to Hyacinth and looked at the muscles in her arms as she worked. I wiped the sweat from my face.

"You from way north, ain't you?" she said. "You come from Iceland?"

"No," I said.

"You look like you do."

She took the coil out. Her skin was smooth and black. "What you staring at?"

"Nothing," I told her.

"I bet there's no colored Eskimos where you come from."

"There's no Eskimos at all."

"You can say that again," she said. She saw me looking at her face, so I dropped my eyes to her red sneakers and kept them there. I could smell her, a sharp, sweet smell.

She turned the coil in her hands. "Hmm," she said. She hefted it. Then she put the coil on the fender. She pulled a wire loose from the engine, took up a wrench, and started working again.

"You know how to play Pigs and Aces?" she asked me. She kept her head under the hood as she worked the wrench.

"No," I told her.

"Figures," she said.

She took out the spark plug. One end was caked black with soot. "Like pulling a bad tooth," she said. She scraped at the black with her thumbnail. "What's wrong with him?"

She looked out at Robert, and I looked, too. He walked along the edge of a cornfield across from the house, working his arms, his hair sticking up. When he got to the end he stopped. Then he turned and came back, slower. His shirt was open halfway down and the bones of his neck and chest showed, even at a distance.

"He's always like that," I told her.

"Yeah?" she said. "He looks like something half-grown, don't he?"

She went in the house.

I looked over at Naomi. When our eyes met, she turned her back to me and ran her hand along the cow's neck.

That time last year when Naomi tried to tell me I didn't understand. It was after he'd had a fight with Ma. Naomi had yelled at him to stop. He called her the same names he was calling Ma.

And then, when Ma went in the other room, he tried to get smart with Naomi. She wouldn't let him touch her. She stayed away from him. But, still, he would bother her.

I heard him tell her once. "You're getting to be a big girl." It was the way he said it, and the way he looked at her when he said it.

He was only trying to be friendly, Ma told her.

Then Naomi started hating Ma for it.

I looked at Robert standing on the edge of the field, then over at Naomi standing near the animals, her back turned on everything. Something in my stomach ached.

* * *

Only Ma and the woman were in the kitchen. I saw a metal table with four old chairs around it, a stove, a cupboard, and shelves full of jars and cans. Ma sat at the table, snapping beans. The woman was at the stove, pouring salt from a cardboard box into a pot.

She was saying, "I been there once, before I married. But this is the best home I know."

Ma looked at me while the woman talked. She was always nervous around people. I sat across from her. Ma said, "It's a nice home you got."

"It does me," the woman answered. She crumbled leaves into the pot. "My girl gets wild sometimes. As you can see."

"She seems like a nice girl," Ma said. Her hands fidgeted even while she worked.

"When she's not a bulldog," the woman answered. She turned from the stove and saw me. "Ain't we all?" She sat down and took up a handful of beans. She put them in my hands with a little push. Then she took some for herself.

We finished without talking. The pot bubbled. I could smell meat. We sat and looked at the beans in the middle of the table. The woman said, "Why don't you put these in now, honey?" I looked up to see if she meant me. Hyacinth stood behind her mother. The girl reached her big arms across the table and lifted the bowl without a sound. I watched as she dumped the vegetables into the pot and stirred.

"You're awfully kind," Ma said. She poked at the collar of her dress. "There's so many of us."

The woman took a stack of dishes from a shelf.

"Is Robert working on the car?" Ma asked me.

"He's not doing anything," I told her.

"Ain't nothing he *can* do," Hyacinth said from the stove.

They sent me to call Robert and Naomi. Naomi went in. Robert stood in front of the car. "I don't go inside no nigger house," he said. "Is that girl going into town for the part?"

"I don't know."

"You send her out here."

"No."

"Who you think you're saying no to?"

I headed for the house.

"You tell your ma I want her," he called.

I kept walking.

"Injun!"

I turned around. "That ain't my name, anyways," I told him, and I went in the house.

Ma and Naomi were at the table. Hyacinth and the woman stood at the stove, talking in low voices. Ma looked over at them while they talked, and she folded the corner of her napkin. When I told her Robert wouldn't come in, she started up from the table. But the woman raised her hand in the air. "Ease your load," she said. "I am sorry if my food isn't suitable for your man." She brought the pot to the table and filled our plates.

"Oh," Ma said, "I'm sure your food is fine." Then she looked down. "He doesn't mean anything by it," Ma told the woman. "He gets moody sometimes. It's because of the car."

"Seem like he's had car trouble a long, long time," Hyacinth said.

"Girl," the woman said to her daughter. Then her

face changed, and the two of them eyed each other, without talking.

The woman said to Ma, "You got your girls here with you. Eat and rest up."

They sat down with us. There were two empty places set.

"Is someone else expected?" Ma asked.

The woman smiled. "Hyacinth, can you pass that bread?" The girl reached her big arm out and handed the bread to her mother.

The woman nodded toward one of the seats. "We keeps that place for my son," she said.

"Mattie," the girl said. "Sometimes he comes here to us."

The woman gazed at her daughter, then nodded. She said to Ma, "He is a miracle, that boy."

The sun was beginning to sink, but it still burned hot and bright across the cornfield and grassy area in front of the house. Hyacinth stood at the pump, washing a tin pail of beets she'd just pulled from the garden. Naomi and I stood barefoot in the puddle, watching. Hyacinth rinsed out the pail, put the cleaned beets in, and filled it with water. "See how it turns pink?" she said. When we bent close to look, she splashed us.

Naomi splashed her back.

Hyacinth straightened up. "So. You alive after all?"

Naomi looked surprised, too. Then she splashed Hyacinth again, and all three of us went at it.

The woman called to her daughter from the porch. "I got to take these in now," Hyacinth said. She drained the water from the pail. "Then I'll go clean up them spark plugs, or you going nowheres." She carried the pail into the house. Her mother sat down on a broken easy chair on the porch.

Naomi and I stood in the cool water. She pushed the wet hair back from her face. Then she carried her shoes over to the tree. She sat down in the shade and started brushing the dirt and grass from her feet.

From her seat on the porch, the black woman watched us—me at the pump, Naomi under the tree, Robert sitting on the car fender, his eyes on Ma.

Ma knelt in front of the porch, at the far end from the woman, pulling weeds from the geraniums and petunias alongside the house. The woman had given her an old straw hat to wear. I watched Ma for a long time. She looked different with the straw hat, kneeling in the dirt. Her dress pulled tight across her back when she reached for a weed. She could have been a stranger. She could have been the one who lived in this house, who worked in her own garden.

I knelt in the sun beside her. Already my clothes were almost dry. Ma didn't look up. She kept working the dirt around the red and white and purple flowers. I could smell them, sharp and sweet. I watched Ma's hands and saw the dirt on them, and the lines. Our hands almost touched. I didn't know what it was I wanted to tell her.

I heard the screen door close. When I looked up, Hyacinth was sitting on the arm of her mother's chair, and they were talking. They stopped and looked our way, then went back to talking. I was embarrassed, thinking they were talking about us, that they knew everything there was to know.

"I want to have a word with you," Robert told Ma.

"I'm busy," Ma said.

"You come with me," he told her. He tried to pull her to her feet.

"Don't act like a fool," Ma told him. She stood up. She looked around to see who was watching. We all were.

"Ma," I said.

"Hush," she told me. "What's happened, Robert? What are you mad at now?"

"Nothing you don't already know about," he told her. "You come to where there ain't no audience and talk."

Ma pulled away from him.

Robert followed her. "You hear me?" he said.

"Stop it," Ma said. She was shouting at him. "Stop it! For God's sake, stop."

Robert backed off. "Okay." He ran his hand through his damp hair. "Okay," Robert said to Ma. He glanced over at the black woman and her daughter. They were standing up like they were ready to come after him. I could see he was afraid of them both. "Don't you think this is the end of it," he told Ma. He turned and walked off across the field.

Ma held her hands folded in front of her. She stood looking out at the trees.

The black woman came down the steps. "Ma'am?" she said.

"It's all right," Ma finally told her.

I helped Ma finish with the flowers.

We were all near the car, Robert, too. The woman told us, "It's too late to fix your car today. You can sleep the night here."

"If your girl don't want to go," Robert said, "I'll go

myself." He looked off to the side of the woman when he spoke.

"The garage is closed now," the woman told him.

"What're you talking about?" Robert said. "She said it's open till dark." He pointed to Hyacinth.

"Used to be," the girl told him.

"Well Christ Almighty," Robert said. "*Used* to be?" He said to the woman, "You sure it's closed?"

"I'm afraid that's right."

He turned on Hyacinth. "What the hell you trying to pull? You know I could've gone myself instead of waiting here for nothing." He walked off a few steps, then came back. "Now what the hell am I going to do?" He looked around at the house, the fields, and the woods. "Why'd you say you was going?"

"I said maybe."

"You little—" Robert moved toward her, then stopped himself. He felt for the cigarettes in his pocket. "We can't stay here," he said. He looked out at the sinking sun. "God Almighty. There's got to be some other place open. I'll go myself right now." His hand shook as he lit the cigarette.

"It's all there is," the woman told him.

Robert looked hard at Hyacinth, like he wanted to hurt her. She bent down to fix her shoelace. "Something's going on here," Robert said. "What the hell's going on?" Then he turned on Ma. "Essie?" he said.

Ma shrugged her shoulders. She looked scared.

"Okay, then," Robert said. "Okay. I'm going myself first thing in the morning. Don't you worry about that."

We left Robert and went inside. Ma was nervous about spending the night, too. She wanted us all to sleep outside in the car.

"There's nothing here to be afraid of," the woman told her. "Don't you know that?"

Ma looked embarrassed. "I know," she said.

They sat at the kitchen table, having tea. Hyacinth took me and Naomi to a wooden box in one corner of the kitchen. She opened the box and showed us the animals she had carved from soap. Naomi fingered the animals. I sat on the floor between the two of them and the women, listening. I didn't care about the animals.

"If you don't mind my asking," the woman said to Ma, "how'd you get with him?"

Ma looked down at her tea.

"I've had my trouble, too," the woman told her. "You wouldn't know it." The woman drank from her cup, then put it down and turned the handle away.

Hyacinth handed Naomi a chunk of soap and a knife. "You want to try?" she asked me.

"No," I said. I rubbed my fingers against the soap rabbit in my hand.

"Your mama ain't going nowhere," Hyacinth told me. She showed Naomi how to carve the soap.

The woman said to Ma, "When she was little." She nodded her head toward Hyacinth. "My boy, Mattie, he was fifteen. There was trouble all the way with him and that man of mine. Finally my boy left home. He went down to Mobile, all by his self, just a baby, too. It was bad between my boy and me. Real bad. He got killed in the train yards."

Ma made a surprised sound. Then she said, "I'm awfully sorry."

The woman nodded. "You know what I'm telling

you." She shook her head. "It was a long, hard time coming to me, though."

Ma looked at the woman, right through her into something else.

Finally Ma said, "It's not like that with Robert."

"No?"

"He's a good man. He was good to me when my husband died. Afterward, too." I thought of the dolls he'd given me and Naomi when we were little, and the rug he got for Ma, and the rosebush. Other things, too, but it didn't matter. There was always a fight in the end.

Ma fidgeted with her cup. She and the woman didn't say anything for a while.

The woman asked her, "How'd your husband die?"

"He was sick," Ma said. They were quiet again. I looked at Naomi and Hyacinth carving the soap.

Ma said, "He loved me, and he loved his babies." She smiled, thinking. "But then he got sick," she said. "And it just got worse. I had to take care of him, and I had to take care of the babies. I couldn't do it," Ma told the woman. "I tried, but then I couldn't do it anymore." She held the teacup between her two hands.

After a while the black woman said, "I see."

Ma took the handkerchief from the sleeve of her dress and wiped her nose.

The woman looked our way, then back at Ma. "How long you all got to pay for it?" she asked.

Ma looked at the woman like she didn't understand. Then she stood up. "You have been kind to us, more than kind, and I thank you." She went to the screen door. "But I won't listen to this," she said, and she went out.

We all looked at the door, the woman, too. Hyacinth said to Naomi, "What you got there, big sister?" She took the soap from Naomi's hand. It was the head of a woman, her long hair falling down in back. "Not bad," Hyacinth said. "Somebody you know?" She gave the soap back to Naomi. We all looked at the door again.

"It's all right," the woman told us. "Don't you worry now."

The woman put blankets down on the kitchen floor for me and Naomi. She told Ma she could sleep on the old couch in her spare room. She didn't tell Robert anything. He started out on the porch, but when the bugs got bad he came inside and went to Ma. I heard her say, "I don't want to talk." Then, "Take my blanket. Go to sleep."

I lay on the floor in the dark and looked at the white light coming through the window. The room was silent. There was a smell of food in the air. I ran my hands along the cool linoleum and felt bread crumbs. Now and then a chicken ruffled its feathers outdoors, or the cow or mule made a noise or moved across the grass.

I thought of Hyacinth living in this odd house. She was black and strong and mysterious to me. I thought of the look on her face when Robert told Ma to stay out of the house. And I thought of the way she smelled when I stood next to her as she worked on the car, a sharp-sweet flower smell.

I drifted off to sleep and dreamed of Hyacinth. We were in a small boat together, riding the waves. Our arms touched. I didn't dare look at her because even with her eyes closed she saw everything. "What you looking at, white girl?" she said to me. "What's *wrong* with you?"

What woke me was a pitiful sound. I thought one of the animals outside had been hurt. But it was coming from Ma's room.

Naomi slept heavily beside me, her breathing steady

like waves. I got to my knees and looked around. The light from the window had shifted, and I did not know what time of night it was. I got up, and when I had stood all the way, the mule's head loomed before me in the window.

I was afraid of seeing Ma like that, crying in the night, but I went into the room just the same. She was in her slip, sitting at one end of the couch. Her hair fell down loose behind her. She was all white—white arms and neck and face and slip—in the dark room. Robert sat on the floor with his face in his hands. He was the one who had been crying, not Ma. Ma's hands rested at her side. Her own face was turned toward the window. Her eyes were closed, as if she were listening to something out there, or else dreaming, while Robert sat with his face in his hands.

He said, "I don't know what gets into me, Es. I can't help it." His voice was thick and far away. "You got to help me."

"I can't help you, Robert," she told him. "I'm tired of this."

"I know," he said. "I know you're tired. But I mean it, Es. I swear this time I mean it. No more fighting. No more—"

"I can't see it, Robert," Ma said. She didn't move a muscle. She didn't open her eyes. "I can't see it at all."

I left the room and lay back down with Naomi. I lay awake a long time, looking at the white light as it entered the window. Then I closed my eyes and tried to think of nothing.

When I woke, Hyacinth was standing over me, laughing. Ma and the woman talked near the stove as they cooked breakfast. Sunlight poured in through the window and screen door.

"Just open up your mouth," Hyacinth told me, "and we'll drop your breakfast down to you." She stepped over me, raising her red high-top sneakers carefully. She wore turquoise pedal pushers with frayed cuffs. When she went out the door, the tails of a man's white dress shirt flapped behind her like wings.

My eyes rested on the small stand near the door. The carved legs shone dark brown in the sunlight. A piece of old newspaper lay folded on the stand, and on it was the coil Hyacinth had taken from the car.

I sat up. Naomi was already gone. Ma turned around, cradling a yellow mixing bowl against her body. She looked fresh and bright, standing in the sunlit room.

"Well," she said. "Did we wake you?"

The black woman winked at me from the stove. "You can fold up them blankets and put them over in the spare room," she told me.

I stood and folded the warm blankets. Ma was telling the woman how she used to fix hair, "before my babies came. Maybe I could open a shop down there in Texas," Ma said.

I held the folded blankets and looked at the two of them. Ma never talked with me and Naomi. She never told us things. I wondered what had happened to make Ma friendly with the woman again.

Ma said, "I'd love to do something like that." She glanced at the woman's hair, then away.

I dumped the blankets on the couch in the spare room. I didn't want to walk back through the kitchen where they were, but it was the only way outside.

Ma said something to the woman about the relatives in Texas. "Are you hungry?" she asked me.

"No," I said.

I went outside. The air and light and the open space all hit me at once, and I felt dizzy. I walked to the tree where the chickens were. I sat on the rusty barrel and looked down at them.

I could not imagine Texas. I tried to think of the home we'd just left, our neighbors, the school. I couldn't see any faces. I couldn't remember the house. I remembered Robert, and Ma and Robert together, fighting. I remembered me and Naomi leaving the house, always leaving, waiting for them to stop. We were both the wrong babies.

And now I was here, nowhere, and Ma and the woman were inside, friendly and talking. When the tears started, I would not wipe them away. I would not touch them. They were not mine.

Naomi walked in front of me and stopped. I kept my hands pressed against the rusted barrel.

The dress hung on Naomi, and her hair fell down in back like Ma's in the night. She was small and thin. She looked like a ghost to me. I knew if I touched her my hand would pass right through her bones and out into air.

I expected her to run from me. But she moved closer, until she almost touched my legs.

"You all right?" Naomi asked me.

I nodded my head yes. I kept nodding my head while she stood there with me.

We ate breakfast without Robert. Hyacinth said, "I wonder if he's started his long walk yet."

"You better go tell him never mind," the woman said.

Ma looked worried.

"He's all right," Hyacinth told her.

Ma fidgeted with her spoon.

The woman took a pan of biscuits from the stove and set them on the table. Hyacinth reached out and took two.

Ma studied Naomi's face while we ate. "Look at those snarls," Ma said.

The sun came through the door behind Naomi, lighting the side of her face and her hair. "I'll have to use that horse brush to get those snarls out," Ma said.

Naomi kept her eyes lowered. I could see she was pleased.

Hyacinth left the table before anyone else, to "go do what I got to," she told us.

As soon as we'd cleaned the breakfast dishes, I went out, too. I stood at the top of the porch steps. Robert was at the shed, with Hyacinth and the mule. He held on to the mule's halter with one hand while he pushed Hyacinth away with the other. She grabbed at the harness that he was trying to hitch to the mule.

The mule ducked its head, then pranced with its back legs. Then it stood still and twitched its ears while Robert and Hyacinth struggled.

I went close to them. "You better let go," I told him. "You better stop it."

"It's this fool girl better let go," he said. "Pretty soon my patience is going to wear out," he told her. "Then I'm gonna break your neck."

She lunged at him and caught him hard across the face with the flat of her hand. "That's it," he said. "You done it now. Injun, hold this mule while I find me a stick."

"No," I told him.

"I said hold him. Or you'll be the same color as her when I'm finished."

"That ain't your mule," I said. "This ain't your house. I don't have to do anything you tell me."

Robert let go of the halter, and he dropped the hand that was holding off Hyacinth. The harness slid to the ground, and the mule nosed at it. Hyacinth stood ready to jump Robert. But Robert looked like the air had just been let out of him.

"Well ain't this a pretty picture?" he said. "Ain't this one son-of-a-goddamn beautiful picture?" Then he turned angry again. "Listen here, I'm not walking nowhere in this heat. I'm taking this mule, you like it or not."

"You don't ride a mule with no plow harness," Hyacinth told him. "Besides, you don't have to go now."

"You been aggravating me since I laid eyes on you," Robert said. He looked her up and down with that look that made me sick. "You could use some straightening out, all right."

She ran her hand along the mule's muzzle. Then she lifted the harness from the ground saying, "Mister, trouble's coming your way."

Robert kept his eyes on the girl. When she turned to carry the harness into the shed, he told me, "Go in the house. This is none of your business."

I walked away a few steps, then stopped to see what would happen. Hyacinth went into the shed. Robert followed her to the doorway and stopped. Then he went inside.

A minute later, Robert jumped back out. He stumbled against the mule, and the mule stepped aside. Hyacinth stood in the doorway and pointed the blade end of a shovel at Robert. He backed up some more.

She didn't look like a girl anymore. She looked old and deep and too mean to tangle with.

Robert watched her, like he was trying to figure her out. Then he laughed and called her a "fool bitch." She swung the shovel across his knees, and he fell to the ground. First he looked dazed. Then his face broke with the pain. He held on to his legs and cried out. Hyacinth stood holding the shovel, watching him.

I thought he was faking. But then I saw he was hurt. I ran to the house and called out for Ma. They all came to the door, and when they saw Robert on the ground and Hyacinth with the shovel, they ran down to see what had happened.

"Get a doctor," Robert kept moaning. "It's broke."

"Hyacinth," the woman said. She raised her arm, as if to shield the girl.

Naomi and I looked at Hyacinth as she stood over Robert with the shovel. When our eyes met hers, all three of us almost laughed, but we stopped ourselves. Hyacinth turned her face away, smiling.

"Robert, what fool thing have you done now?" Ma said. She looked down at him. Her face turned cold, like she was just seeing something. "Robert, I cannot stand for any more of this," she said.

"My leg," he said.

She knelt down, with that look on her face. When she touched his leg, he cried out.

Ma and the woman lifted Robert under the arms and moved him to the shade tree. He wouldn't let them take him in the house.

"Don't break my arm, too," he told the woman. He leaned back against the tree and held his legs.

The woman looked hard at Robert. Then she told Ma, "I will be back shortly."

"Bring me some whiskey," Robert told her. Hyacinth followed her mother into the house.

Robert quieted down after a while.

"Do you want to try to stand?" Ma asked him.

"Get me the hell out of here," he told her.

"I wish I could do that," she said. Her face was like stone.

We waited for the woman to return. Robert sat with his eyes closed, moaning. "I'll kill that bitch," he said. His head rested against the tree. His face was flushed and sweating.

When the woman came back she handed Robert a cup.

Robert tasted it and spit it out. "Tea?" he said. "Get me out of here."

Hyacinth returned, too, and stood next to her mother.

"What the hell you all standing around for?" Robert said.

The woman told Ma, "I am fixing you some food to take."

"Take?" Ma said.

Hyacinth nodded toward Robert and said to Ma, "There's a doctor in town. Or else the hospital is an hour and a half more."

Ma looked at her and shook her head.

"You can drive, can't you?" Hyacinth said.

"Is the car running?" Ma asked.

"It's fixed," Hyacinth told her.

"I told you the son of a bitches were up to no good," Robert said. The black woman looked hard at him.

"I don't understand," Ma said. "We can leave, then?" she asked the girl. Then, "Robert, are you able to move?"

"Get me the hell out of here," he said again. He

tried to push himself up from the tree, but he fell back.

"How'd it get fixed," Ma said, "without the new part?" "Did you fix it?"

"I told you they were lying," Robert said.

Hyacinth motioned for me to help Ma get Robert to his feet. Ma pulled on one side and I pulled on the other. "What for?" Robert asked the woman and her daughter. "What I ever do to you?"

We got him to the car. Ma had him get in the backseat, where he'd have more room. "You brought this on yourself," she told him.

We left Robert groaning in the car and followed the black woman into the house. I helped her wrap the food in waxed paper. She put a loaf of bread and cheese into a brown paper bag. I looked over at the stand near the door, the one where the broken car part had been. In place of the coil and folded newspaper was a potted geranium, its flowers bright red in the sunlight.

The woman said, "Ma'am, you will do fine where you go."

Ma stared hard at the food on the table. She said, "He's a good man. I want you to know that. Somewhere inside him, he's a good man."

The woman straightened up and looked a long time at Ma. "There's plenty crying to be saved," she said. "Why you working so hard on one who don't want it?"

Ma shook her head. Then she said, "Maybe he does want it."

"Maybe," the woman said. "But it looks to me like you have done what you can do. The horse knows by now where the water is. If he won't drink of it, that's between him and God." She folded shut the paper bag. She said, "Be thankful you got your babies here." She stretched her arms out toward me and Naomi. I could almost feel her hand touch my shoulder.

The sun was high and bright. The mule and cow stood near the shed, grazing. Robert sat with his legs drawn up onto the backseat. He looked out and was quiet.

Ma said, "Audrey, Naomi. I want you girls to get in front."

"You want me to?" I said.

I got in the front seat, between Ma and Naomi.

Hyacinth poked her head in the window. She winked, first at me, then at Naomi, with her big, shiny, serious face. "Stay smart," she told us. Naomi lowered her eyes to the paper bag at her feet.

The black woman stood on the other side of the car. She squeezed Ma's hand good-bye.

Ma started the car. It sputtered, but it stayed running. Ma pulled the car out the long driveway. The sun burned down on the white road, making it shimmer. When we turned onto the paved road, I looked back. They were all there, standing in a circle of green—the woman, the girl, the animals.

Hyacinth raised her hand to wave at us, and the woman, too, waved.

We headed down the road. We were quiet for a while. Then Robert moaned. He said, "Where you taking me?"

"I will take you to a hospital," Ma said.

"That's all I need now is a broken leg."

Ma looked into the rearview mirror at him. "Robert," she said, "I don't know what's going to happen to you."

"What you talking about?" he said. He laughed. Then his voice got worried. "What do you mean, Es?"

Ma looked up into the mirror again. Then she looked straight ahead at the road while she drove.

"Essie," Robert said.

"Robert, the girls and I are going to stay with my cousin."

"Cousin? What cousin?" he said. "Where? What are you talking about?"

"I'm taking the car. You'll manage. You always do."

"What the hell are you talking about?" Robert said. "Goddamnit. Essie."

Ma didn't answer. She kept driving.

I could feel him in the backseat, staring at her. I was afraid to turn and look at him, afraid to see his face. For a minute, I felt sorry for him. But then my throat tightened, and everything fell away.

Naomi nudged me. "Show her," she said. She put the carved soap in my hand. I held it for a minute, feeling its smoothness. Then I handed it to Ma.

BREAD

So still and cool, everything, with the sunlight coming through the bedroom window, and the dust moving in the beam of sunlight. She could see the dust. At the hospital everything was white—or steel, if that was a color. And the air was empty. Here the air was full, and there were colors: pink and yellow in the curtain, and a pale blue wall. But the colors seemed out of place.

She smelled sauce. Yesterday her mother told her father on the way home, "You'd better get an extra pound of macaroni."

He muttered under his breath about it. "That's what Josie wants," her mother said to him, "so you be quiet about it."

After the hospital, it had felt so queer riding in the car, with the hollow sound of the tires going around and around on the pavement, and the loud engine, and everything flashing by.

When she got home, she lay down on the couch. Her mother turned on the TV and covered her with a blanket. Josie heard her brothers arguing in the hall on their way outdoors, and the TV getting louder and softer. Everything got louder and softer. She was tumbling through air.

And then she woke up in her bed and it was Sunday morning. When she tried to get out of bed, the pain jumped in her side. She put her hand over the scar. It didn't hurt so much.

She could have died.

She could have died, she thought, and that funny feeling went through her stomach again. But her dresser was there, and the lamp, and the books.

She heard voices downstairs—her father and mother and once in a while her brothers. Mostly she heard pans and dishes.

Her mother hadn't called to her this morning, "Josie! You'll make us late for church." And now it must be almost noon.

She got out of bed. She had never noticed how big her room was. Her bathrobe hung on the bedpost, and she put it on. But she couldn't find her slippers. She looked under the bed. There was nothing there, not even dust.

Poison, they had said. The nurse told her it was like pus. If the appendix exploded, the poison went all through your body and you were dead. Last year, when Robbie got the sliver in his foot, the doctor used tweezers to take it out, and gave him a shot to make the pus go away.

But this was different. This was inside and tweezers couldn't take it out. Robbie had run barefoot over old boards. What had she done?

She peered into the mirror. How spooky she looked, with the robe hanging open and her hair flying every which way, and her eyes round and dark, as if they belonged to somebody else.

Usually she dressed as soon as she got up. But today it didn't seem right. At the hospital everyone wore gowns and white robes, all day long, even the doctors and nurses. They reminded her of angels.

And she had missed the church play. Nobody said a word about it, either, all the time she was in the hospital, and she had been afraid to ask. She was supposed to be the angel who said "Glory, Glory, Glory" when they crowned Mary. Her mother had finished making the angel's wings just in time. And then Josie got sick.

She could just hear what her mother had to say about it, how she had to find somebody at the last minute to take Josie's place, how it was always one thing after another.

But she hadn't meant to get sick.

She had seen the hospital from the outside lots of times. She couldn't have imagined what was in there, though: so many beds and curtains and people; metal sounds and beeps and footsteps; all those TVs going, and stretchers and carts clanging through the halls, day and night.

The other girls in her ward showed her their scars and parts of their bodies that she'd always been told were private. And sometimes they used bedpans.

Then Josie had to use the bedpan, too.

But it was nothing. It was nothing because they were all there together, and the doctor came in and called her "Chickadee," and the nurse bent over and smiled, and the high school girl chewed bubble gum and brought them cards and flowers.

The other girls had their stuffed animals and dolls with them.

"Will you bring my doll?" Josie asked her mother.

"What do you want that for? You'll lose it," her mother answered. "Somebody will steal it on you."

She talked so loud that Josie was embarrassed.

"But I want it."

"Don't think I'm getting you another one if you lose this one," her mother said. "I don't want to hear about it if you lose it."

But she hadn't lost it. Josie picked up the doll from the chair next to her dresser. Then she remembered: *That's* where her costume had been hanging the night she got sick.

She smoothed the doll's dress and lay her down in the warm bedcovers. She tucked the covers around her doll. Then she stepped out into the hall.

A chickadee was a bird.

Her side ached when she walked. When she flushed the toilet, her mother called from far away, "Josephine, is that you?"

Josie stopped at the head of the stairs and rested her hand on the cool, smooth railing. The bottom looked so far away. Every time she let herself down a step, she felt a tug in her side.

Robbie and Al sprawled in the living room watching the Tarzan movie. She only saw their legs when she went by the door, and parts of the Sunday comics. They hadn't come to visit her. They hadn't even come to say hello when she got home yesterday.

The funny thing was, she had been feeling so well at the hospital. But now she felt groggy, like right after the operation. And the house seemed so big.

But the air felt warmer as she got closer to the kitchen, and that made her feel better.

She stopped in the doorway, startled. A hulking grizzly bear, dressed in a blue suit, sat at the kitchen table.

But it was only her father, with his ledger and paper and pencil. He glanced at her. "She's up," he said, and then he wrote something in the ledger.

Josie's mother stood on her step stool in front of the stove. She looked over her shoulder at Josie. "Good," she said, but she didn't sound very happy about it. She turned back to stirring the pot of sauce. "We thought you were going to sleep all day."

Josie watched her mother's shoulders move. She was almost as short as Josie. But strong, like a boxer. "A solid woman," that's what her father called her.

One nurse called Josie "Honey." Another called her "Sweetie." They used such funny names there.

Her mother looked around at her again. "You better put something on your feet."

"Christ," her father said. He bent close to the table and erased something from the ledger. Then he wrote something else down.

Josie and her mother and brothers always went to early Mass together so that her mother could get back to cook. Her father went alone later at ten. But Josie and her brothers knew he didn't go to church, even though he put his suit on, because they'd had to go with him when their mother had the flu. The first time he left them off and picked them up afterward. The other time he took them right to the diner and they ate pancakes with syrup while their father drank coffee and made smart remarks to everybody.

"What kind of sin is it," Josie had asked her mother, "if you're on your way to church but don't get there, but it's not your fault?"

"Don't talk such foolishness," her mother scolded.

And now Al and Robbie wanted to go to church with their father all the time, but their mother wouldn't let them.

"Do you hear me?" her mother said. "Put something on your feet."

How could Josie tell her that she hadn't lost the doll, but she'd lost the slippers?

"Does your operation hurt?" her mother asked.

"No."

"That's good." She reached to the back of the stove and took the lid off the pot of water to check it.

"I hope you're hungry," she said. "There's lots to eat."

Once Josie's friend Evelyn slept over. When she saw Josie's mother on the step stool, cooking dinner, she clapped her hand over her mouth and ran out of the room. "A witch," Evelyn giggled. Josie laughed with her a little bit. Then Evelyn had to hurry to the bathroom because she was going to wet her pants from laughing, and Josie stood in the hallway digging her fingernails into her arms while she waited for the door to open again.

Her father slapped his hand on the table. "That does it," he said. "I have to get rid of the Lorelli kid."

Her mother let out a sigh.

"He takes the truck for a job and then goes driving all over hell," her father said. "I'm losing money."

He shook his head and looked straight at Josie. "What can I do?" he asked. "I've got a business to run, don't I?"

The Lorellis were her father's friends. Everybody was her father's friend. But nobody knew how to work for him.

Right before Christmas, Josie's mother and father had had a fight. Now he had to hand over all his money as soon as he got it so Josie's mother could pay the bills. "It's either that, or there's the door," she told him. She stood in front of him, pointing her finger as she talked, and her dark hair bounced every time she pointed. She only came up to his chest.

"You run everything else," he shouted back at her. "You may as well run this, too."

"Thank God *somebody* in this house knows how to run things," she said, "or we'd all be out on the street."

Now her father shook his head at Josie. "You can't be a boss and a nice guy, too." That's what he always said. He picked up the ledger and waved it in the air. "See what I get? I'm going broke, that's what."

"If it wasn't for me," Josie's mother said, "you'd be worse than broke." She turned and gave him that look. "If it wasn't for me, you know where you'd be with that business of yours."

Her father dropped the ledger on the table. He threw both hands up in the air and leaned back in his seat. Then he dropped his hands on the table. "Do you know how much that hospital room cost for *one day*, for Christ's sake?"

Josie waited for him to answer, but he didn't say how much it cost.

"What the hell." He pushed the ledger away and reached for part of the Sunday paper.

Her mother lifted the lid and dumped a handful of salt in. Every once in a while she'd start to hum, a few notes that weren't even a tune. She'd catch herself and stop. But then she'd start up again, the same few notes that didn't sound like anything.

That funny feeling in Josie's stomach wouldn't go away. It wasn't the operation: something else. Like when she watched a parade and the drums went by, booming so hard that they shook her insides, and she had to wrap her arms around herself and hold on.

"Get the napkins, will you?" her mother said to her, and suddenly she felt a little better.

When Josie opened the cupboard behind her father he said, "She doesn't look so good."

She turned to see what he meant.

Her mother shrugged. "What do you expect?" she said. She went to the refrigerator and took out the dish of grated cheese and set it on the table, next to the stack of plates and silverware. She moved the loaf of bread Josie's father had picked up at the bakery that morning and put it on the table.

"Clear those things away," she told Josie's father. She pushed the newspaper and ledger in front of him.

Then she raised the back of her hand to Josie's forehead, so quickly that it made Josie's head jerk back. Her mother's dark eyes burned a hole right through her. Josie looked into those eyes, afraid of what her mother was finding out.

"Tie your bathrobe," she said. "Before you trip and break your neck."

Josie looked down at the belt trailing on the floor.

And then the lid on the pot started clanging and her mother hurried back up the stool.

There had been that odd night in the hospital when visiting hours were over but her mother stayed. She stood by the bed, looking at Josie for the longest time, and her face was soft and puffy, like something was happening to it. She leaned over the bed railing toward her, and just before their faces touched, her mother straightened up. She patted the railing so hard that the bed shook. "I'll see you tomorrow," she said. She said it again, and left.

Her mother dumped the macaroni into the boiling water and stirred. "Nick," she told Josie's father, "get those boys in here to set the table."

"God Almighty," he said. He stood and swept the papers and ledger together and carried them out of the room.

"You're not supposed to be on your feet like that after an operation," her mother told her. "Sit down and fold the napkins."

Josie put her own hand to her forehead. The skin felt cool. She was sure it was supposed to feel warm. Warm or hot.

"*You* set the table," Al shouted to Robbie in the next room.

They were always fighting. And Robbie hated her, and she hadn't done a thing. It was because he had to share a room with Al. "I don't see why *she* gets her own room," he cried to their parents. When no one was looking, he would punch her arm.

If she cried, her father started yelling: "I should get rid of all three of you. I should rent your rooms out and get something back for all my trouble."

And then her mother would answer him, "If anybody moves out I can tell you right now who it's going to be. I can tell you right now who should be getting something back for all her trouble."

It was usually Josie's job to set the table, but her

mother had told her to get the napkins. And sit down.

"I had to go to three different stores to get the pudding you like," her mother told her. "And I got your whipped cream, too."

But Josie didn't care about pudding and whipped cream. She wanted to know what had happened to her costume.

Her mother sighed again, louder. "*I* should have been the one to stay in the hospital."

Before the operation, Josie had never stayed away from home for even one night. She was afraid to sleep in a strange place. Even when the pain in her stomach got so bad that she couldn't stand up, she begged them to let her stay home. But then everything happened so fast, and they gave her the operation, and she didn't have time to think about it.

Now she was back home, and she wanted to cry.

"Nick, boys," her mother called out. She spooned a piece of macaroni from the pot and blew on it, then popped it into her mouth. Josie could tell by the way her mother's hair moved that she was chewing hard and fast—like she did everything.

"What did you do with my—?" Josie blurted. "The angel wings," she said.

Her mother turned and gave her a terrible look. But then she turned back to the stove. "I gave everything to the nuns. Let them worry about it."

And that was that.

The slippers weren't really part of the costume, even though her mother had said she could wear them in the play. But her mother must have given the slippers away. She couldn't have, Josie thought, and she looked at her, trying to figure it out.

A *witch*, her friend Evelyn had said. But she was wrong. Except that her mother knew everything, if that's what being one meant.

When Josie's grandmother died, everybody at the funeral home said how awful she looked. "What do you expect?" her mother told them. And then she acted like everything was so very normal, and nothing at all was changed, while Josie's grandmother lay stiff under a pile of smelly flowers. Her mother knelt in front of the casket a long time. Then she patted her grandmother's dress and got up fast and left. Later, they gave away all her clothes.

"Are you folding those napkins?" her mother said. "You better fold a few extra ones."

"Why?" Josie wanted to know.

"So we'll have them," her mother said.

Josie watched her mother stir the sauce. The way her arms moved back and forth from one big pot to another reminded her of a policeman directing traffic.

And then the truth hit her, so hard that she had to catch her breath. Her mother had cooked too much, just like last year when everybody came to their house after the funeral. She had known what had happened to her all along, even when Josie was in the hospital, but wouldn't tell her.

Pretty soon they'd have to say it, though. And then Robbie would get her room.

But when he moved into her room, what would happen to her?

Josie's legs felt funny. She sat down at the table. Everything was so bright: the bright plates and silverware, the light reflecting off the shiny tabletop, the white napkins, the white bread wrapper.

She could smell the bread. The curved end of the loaf

stuck out of its wrapper, and she touched it. It was warm. Sometimes she went to the bakery with her father, and he always bought her something for a treat.

She edged the loaf out of the wrapper and tried to break off a little piece. But the bread was soft and mashed in her hands. She looked over to see if her mother was watching.

Josie got the piece off. She popped it into her mouth, and as soon as she started chewing she realized how hungry she was.

Josie broke off another piece. The bread tasted sweet and made her feel warm, the way she felt when she curled up under the covers on her bed. It was almost like being in a dream.

She looked out from the dream and saw her mother take up the pot holders, lift the heavy pot, and carry it down the step stool and over to the sink. The steam trailed behind her in slow white curls, like funny long antlers. She glanced at Josie, then dumped the water into the colander. A cloud of steam rose up and covered her face.

But the bread wasn't going anywhere; Josie couldn't feel it in her stomach. She broke off another piece, and this time she hardly chewed before she swallowed. She had to hold the loaf in both hands to pull the pieces off. And while she ate she watched her mother and thought of how everyone was pretending she'd had the operation in time.

But she didn't feel any way at all about it.

The cloud broke apart, and her mother's face came back, first one part, then another. When the whole face was there, she looked like she wanted to run at Josie and grab her. But her hands were full, so she couldn't move.

"Nick," she called.

Josie turned to see, but her father wasn't in the room.

Her mother called again, louder, "Nick, come here." She held the pot in her hands while she watched the doorway.

"Nick!" her mother called, and at last her father hurried into the room.

"What the hell?" he said. "What happened?"

Her mother motioned at Josie with her chin. "Look at her," she said. "Make her stop."

So it was happening. She was starting to go, even though she didn't want to.

"Nick," her mother said. "For God's sake, I've only got two hands."

Her father straightened up and gave her the queerest look. He walked over and touched her shoulder, but she couldn't feel a thing.

"Honey," he said. "What are you doing?"

Everything was all mixed up. He never called her "Honey."

Let him, she thought. If they really wanted her they could have thrown their arms around her and held on. They could have made her stay. It didn't matter, though, because she wasn't going to leave, even if she was dead. She tore at the bread.

"Honey, why are you doing that?" he asked. He reached his hand out toward her.

But she pulled back and held on. She kept eating.

She wasn't going to let him take the bread from her. She wasn't going to let them take anything.

MUSKRAT

They were going to trap for muskrat because Carr's Hardware was paying seventy-five cents
a pelt. But they only had two traps and all the stores
were sold out. The one place left to get traps was from
Charlie Coe.

They walked to Charlie Coe's, but they did not stop
at the little house where his mother lived. Instead, they
followed the two-by-eights that led over the mud to
Charlie Coe's shack behind his mother's house. The
younger boy thought they should turn back. The older boy

laughed and called him "Scaredy." There was chicken wire over the windows of the shack, and dirty plastic over the wire, so they could not see in. They stood there looking at the door, not knowing if they should knock or call out. They could hear pigeons. Then Charlie Coe opened the door. They looked at his bald head and his smooth white skin.

"What are you looking for?" he asked them.

"Muskrat traps," they said.

"There's no muskrat traps here," he told them.

"Old Man Carr said you had some," the older boy said.

The boys kept looking at his bald head and his pale skin. His eyes seemed almost pink.

Charlie Coe pulled the door open and told the boys to come in. They heard pigeon sounds and rustling. Then he closed the door. A light bulb hung from the ceiling. They could see wooden boxes nailed to the walls and inside the boxes, pigeons. They saw the unlit iron stove with a soup can on top of it. They saw the army cot near the window, and on it, an open magazine.

"Maybe I got one or two left," Charlie Coe told them. He knelt alongside the cot and began looking through a box of junk. Then without looking up he reached onto the cot for the magazine. His hand touched the woman on the page as he closed it and turned it over.

They stared at him as he looked through the box of junk. They stared at his bald head because Charlie Coe was not an old man or any kind of man. He had just quit high school.

"There's nothing in here," he told them.

He stood up and felt along the top of a row of pigeon nests. He put his hand into one of the boxes and smoothed the feathers on the bird. "She's been laying," he told them.

The younger boy looked at his older friend. Russell jammed his fists into his pockets and nodded, squinting his eyes, as if he understood, as if he and Charlie Coe were talking men's talk.

Charlie Coe went over to the other wall and felt along the top of the boxes. He pulled down a rusty trap. "I knew that bastard was in here somewhere," he said. He held it by the chain in front of the two boys. "How much you got?" he asked them.

"It's too rusty," the older boy said. "It won't work."

Charlie Coe handed it to him. "Try it."

Russell bent over and pushed his foot down on the trap, but it would not open. Then the younger boy, Tim, tried. "Ain't you ever worked a trap before?" Charlie Coe asked them. "Ain't you ever trapped?" He laughed. "A couple of greenhorns?"

"The trap's no good," Russell told him. He didn't want Charlie Coe thinking he was a greenhorn.

Charlie Coe took it from them. He held it in one hand and opened it. They looked at his big pink hand and wrist. He put the trap on the floor. He broke a piece of wood from one of the boxes and touched the wood to the center of the trap. It sprang, making a thwacking sound, and bounced against the floor. They looked at the closed trap with the piece of wood caught in it.

"You put a little machine oil on it," Charlie Coe said. "Rust ain't nothing. How much you got?"

"We'll give you a quarter," Russell said.

Charlie Coe made a noise that sounded like he was trying to laugh. "I'll take seventy-five cents."

"They hardly cost more than that new," Tim said.

"Get one new," Charlie Coe told him.

They took money from their pockets and stood together whispering. They gave the money to Charlie Coe and he gave them the trap.

"You want to buy a pigeon?" Charlie Coe asked them. He went to one of the boxes and lifted out a bird. He put it on the cot. The bird arched its neck and stuck its tail feathers into the air.

"What's wrong with it?" Tim asked.

"Didn't you ever see a fantail?" Charlie Coe said. He picked up the pigeon and held it. He made a noise to it with his tongue and the bird pecked his finger. He put the bird near his face and called it "Baby."

He put the pigeon back, took out another, and held it close to his jacket. "I can show you something," Charlie Coe told them. "This is an eight-dollar bird." He took them outside and closed the door.

They looked at him in the bright outside light. They saw the fine white fuzz on the top of his head when he bent his head over the pigeon.

"I know you never seen this," Charlie Coe said. He tossed the bird above his head. It fluttered, then flew away.

"Why you letting him go?" Tim asked.

"It's a homing pigeon, dummy," Russell told him. He looked at Charlie Coe and nodded, proud of their shared knowledge.

"Any bird's a homing bird if you feed it," Charlie Coe said. "Watch it." He pointed.

They looked at the bird as it climbed.

"How high does he go?" Tim asked. He swung the trap and the rust came off on his hand.

"See?" Charlie Coe said. "You watching?"

They looked up again. The bird was falling. "What happened to it?" Tim asked. "Did somebody shoot it?" They stared at the bird as it tumbled down.

"He's going to crash," Russell said, and he became as excited as Tim. "Look at him. Look at him. Is he dead?"

Then the bird was flying again. Russell's face turned red and he looked away. Tim looked at Charlie Coe.

"I knew you never seen anything like that," Charlie Coe told them. The bird flew back and landed on the ground near them. "I just got three of them hatched," Charlie Coe said. "I got any kind of pigeon you want."

"I don't want any pigeons," Russell told him.

"I don't think we got a place to keep them," Tim said.

They started walking back over the wood planks to the road.

"I can sell you a regular pigeon for a dollar," Charlie Coe called after them.

They were on the road walking home. The younger boy, Tim, was swinging the trap. Then he began dragging it.

"Don't drag it," Russell told him.

"We got gypped," Tim said.

"We got to get one muskrat to pay for that trap," Russell said. "Then we'll start making money."

"How come he doesn't have any hair?" Tim asked.

"I think he was born that way," Russell said. "I don't know."

They walked along the road. Tim started dragging the trap again. "Did you see it when it fell?" he asked.

They went to Russell's barn and worked on the trap, cleaning it, oiling it, working it. They took the other two traps with them and set off for the ditch.

It was a deep trough the farmers had dug, to drain their fields. The boys stumbled down the overgrown bank. They found a couple of runs in the shallow water, where the ditch broadened and became almost creeklike, with a silty bottom. They set the traps, and pushed a sturdy piece of wood through each end ring, deep into the ground. They noticed the burrows in the sides of the bank and talked about the good spot they had found, knowing what they knew from reading or listening to others talk of trapping. Then, as they followed the ditch, walking through the water in their boots, looking for a place to set the last trap, Tim pointed to the ground and they bent over to look. They saw bird tracks, but among them were the distinct prints of an animal. "Muskrat," Russell said, although there was no way for either of them to know a muskrat print from a weasel or opossum or raccoon. Except, they knew, it was not rabbit or cat or dog.

They had never been this far down the ditch before. "What's that noise?" Tim asked.

Russell looked around. "What noise?" He laughed at Tim. "You scared, little baby?"

"I just wondered what it was." Tim walked faster, swinging his arms, taking the lead. Russell stayed behind him and kept looking around as they walked.

At one point, where the bank had been eroded so that nothing grew, not even briars, they discovered a large burrow. It had been dug into the sandy bank below the remains of an old tree stump.

"Look at the size of that muskrat hole," Tim said.

"Maybe it's a woodchuck hole," Russell said.

"This close to the water?"

"It could be."

"It could be a giant muskrat," Tim said. "Or something else big. What else could it be?"

Russell shook his head. They went near the hole and peered in. But they could not see anything.

They set the last trap, the one they had got from Charlie Coe, in a place where the water narrowed into a six-inch channel and the mud spread out on either side, smooth and unbroken.

"We don't keep anything in our old shed anymore," Tim said. "I bet I could use that."

"What for?"

"Pigeons," Tim said. "I'm going to get some."

"What do you want with pigeons?"

"I just want some."

"Charlie Coe's pigeons?" Russell asked. "You going to start buying pigeons from Charlie Coe now?"

Then they were done and they walked back through the ditch to look at their traps. "I could quit school when I'm sixteen," Russell said.

"No you can't. Your mother and father won't let you."

"They can't stop me," Russell said. "Let them try." He kicked at a stone in his path. "I'll go up to Canada and fish and trap all day, do whatever I want." He kicked the stone out of his path and lost it. "You can come. But you'll have to wait till you're old enough."

"Me too," Tim said. "I'm quitting, too."

They went home talking of trapping and pelts and money, lots of money, of becoming trappers, of cutting trees, maybe, and building a cabin.

They ran to the ditch the next afternoon, expecting to find all three traps sprung and heavy with animals. But there was nothing. The clear water trickled over the undisturbed silty bottom, and the bare mud along the banks remained unmarred except for the same cluster of bird and animal prints.

"Maybe we should use some bait," Tim said.

"My father said you don't have to," Russell told him. "Just put the traps in those runs they have to swim through."

"Old Man Carr uses apple chunks with cinnamon."

"We don't need bait."

"If we don't catch anything tomorrow I'm bringing some apples," Tim said.

The next day they could see before they reached it that the first trap had been sprung. But it was empty. They searched for tracks.

"Maybe the water's too deep here," Russell said.

"But we almost got him," Tim said.

They headed for the second trap.

"I bet the other trap got him," Tim said.

It had not been sprung.

"I'm coming back later with apples," he said. "We got to use bait. You got any cinnamon at your house?"

"I think so," Russell said.

They headed for the last trap. At first they could not find where they had left it. Then they realized it was gone. "The stick, too," Tim said. "Somebody stole it."

"I bet it was one of those Housemans," Russell said. "If I catch one of those Housemans down here I'll kill him."

They found no tracks. The hole in the mud where the stick had been was widened as if the stick had been worked around in it.

"Just let me catch one of those Housemans," the boy said.

"Maybe they're still down here," Tim said.

They stopped looking when they passed the burrow under the stump on the eroded bank. A stick was caught across the opening. They saw the metal ring on it and a few links of chain disappearing into the hole.

"We got a muskrat," Tim said. "We finally got one. I knew we'd get one."

They stood in front of the hole and listened. "Maybe he's dead," the boy said.

"We got to pull him out," Russell said.

"Do they bite?" Tim asked.

Russell picked up the stick and chain and pulled. "It's a big one," he said. "God, it won't budge."

They pulled together, slipping on the bank, making the dirt roll down into the ditch bottom. Each time they edged the animal forward a few inches it pulled itself back in. They pushed the end of the stick into the dirt so the animal could not get away, and they rested.

"What is it?" Tim asked.

"It's too big for a muskrat," Russell said. "It's too strong."

"How we going to get it out?" They stared at the hole. "Maybe we should leave him here," Russell said. "He'll die."

"We could pull him out and club him," Tim said. He looked around for a piece of wood.

"We can't pull him out," Russell said. "Maybe if we come back tomorrow we can get him."

"I can pull him out," Tim said. He had found a big piece of wood for a club. "I'm going to get him."

"Go ahead. But he's too strong."

Tim dropped his club and pulled the stick from the dirt. He held the chain and began tugging. Russell watched, offering advice and orders from time to time.

Tim grunted. "You're just scared of it."

"I am not scared," Russell answered.

Tim fell onto his knees. "Help me," he called.

They pulled together on the chain. Slowly they worked the animal out. They could see its brown fur, but they could not tell what it was.

"I think I got him," Tim said. "Get that club. When I pull him out, get ready." Russell found the club and put it within reach, then helped pull again.

They got the animal out. It was big—bigger than a cat. Russell grabbed the club and raised it. The animal looked at him, glassy-eyed, not moving. "It's not a muskrat," Russell said, the club still raised. They stood, one holding the club, the other holding the chain, waiting.

"What is it?" Tim asked.

"Maybe it's a weasel," Russell answered.

The trap had got the animal high on the back leg. It lay motionless, except for its silent, heavy breathing. The boy touched the stick to the animal's face, but it did not move. It followed the stick with its glassy eyes.

"What shall we do with him?" Tim asked.

"Just get the trap off."

"I'm not touching him. He'll bite," Tim said.

"If I could knock him out," Russell said, "we could take the trap off." He looked at the animal as he rolled the stick in his hands. "He's too big."

They decided to drag the animal behind Russells's barn. There they planned to kill it with rocks and pieces of cinder block. Russell lifted it by the chain, but when the animal jerked around suddenly he jumped and dropped it. The younger boy scrambled for the chain and lifted the animal, holding it by the chain at arm's length. "You better carry him," Russell told the younger boy.

"So I can get him with the club if he tries to get away."
They walked fast, but Tim had to keep stopping to rest
his arms. Every now and then the animal jerked and
twisted and they would jump back from it without letting go. Russell carried the stick, keeping his eyes on the
animal.

They staked it behind the barn, knocking the wood
deep into the ground with a rock. "You going to hit him?"
Tim asked.

Russell held a rock. "I don't know," he said. "You
want to do it?"

They looked at the animal's face. "Maybe we can leave
him for a while," Russell said, "and he'll just die."

They gathered rocks and pieces of cinder block and
piled them on the animal to keep him from getting away.
The animal watched them with its quiet, glassy eyes. Its
breathing had slowed. They watched him until it was too
dark to see. Then they raced home.

They came back the next morning before school. The
animal looked dead, but when they poked it with a stick
its eyes moved. "How can he still be alive?" Russell said.

"Is he going to starve to death?" Tim asked. "Or die
of thirst?"

"He's supposed to be dead," Russell said.

"Maybe we can let him go," Tim said. "Can't we?"

"It's too late. He's mad now. He'll go wild and attack
us. We'll get rabies."

"We should have left him where we found him," Tim
said. "We should have taken the trap off and let him go."

They piled more rocks on the animal and left for
school.

*   *   *

When they came back that afternoon they were sure it was dead. "He suffocated," Tim said. "We crushed him."

"It's about time," Russell said.

"Do you think we crushed its chest?" Tim asked. "That's how Cliff Pratt's father died—of a crushed chest." He put his own hand to the front of his jacket.

They stared at the animal's face, its eyes dulled and half-opened. The pile of rocks covered all but the head and part of the chain.

"Let's get rid of him," Russell said. They kicked the rocks away from the animal. They kept looking at its eyes.

"How come he's watching us if he's dead?" Tim asked.

"Hurry up," Russell told him. They finished removing the rocks.

"Look," Tim said. He was bent over and pointed. "He crapped under all those rocks. Is that what that stuff is?" He laughed, then stopped.

"Holy God," Russell said. He leaned over Tim's shoulder and looked. "Holy God. Let's get him out of here." He worked the stick out of the ground.

"What about the trap?" Tim asked.

They looked at the animal, at the trap clamped high on its leg. They saw the half-opened eyes that seemed to be watching them.

"It was your idea," Tim said. "You said we could make money." He backed off, his hand on the front of his jacket.

Russell picked up the chain. He headed for a clump of weeds, moving fast, dragging the animal. Tim followed. Russell hurled the animal into the dead weeds and brush. It made a crashing sound as it tumbled into the dead weeds. Without waiting to see where it landed, the boys turned and ran. They headed for a corn stubble field and crossed it, racing, until they reached another field. They gave their secret war cry, shrill and loud, and it pierced the air and carried. They hooted it over and over as they ran, first one, then the other, then together. They kept racing. When they reached the row of trees that bordered Tim's yard, they were breathless and exhausted, and when it seemed they could not go any farther, they kept racing.

EMERGENCY

After Mrs. Woody's husband died and her only son, Roy, left for business college, she began laying up her treasure. She turned fanatic about saving as much as she could each month from her social security check, and hoarded every little thing that came her way, all in preparation for that terrible time—which she said she hoped never came but which, in fact, she lived for—when a real emergency hit. The inside of her house started to look like a junkyard.

Roy knew she had nearly seven hundred dollars

stuffed in the rusted coffee can at the back of her clothes wardrobe. He'd seen it, after he'd come back home from college, when he went looking through her closets for things he and Candy could use in their new apartment. The sight of all that money shocked him at first. Then the money got into his blood.

"At least," he kept telling her, "buy yourself a good winter coat. Look at that rag of yours." He pointed to the limp cloth that hung on the kitchen rack among an assortment of ladies' belts tied in a bundle, a nylon bag stuffed full of hats, and a tangled Chinese wind chime. She had taken the coat out to brush it off and "get it ready."

In fact, she had been thinking for a while now that she needed a new coat. But the thought of spending any of her money sent a little shudder through her. After all, she could go on wearing a sweater underneath. Then, if anything came up, she'd still have her money.

"What could come up?" he asked.

"You never know."

"One damn coat," he said. "It's not like I'm asking you to sink your whole life savings into something foolish."

She eyed him, wondering what he knew about life savings.

He tried to explain to her about investments, how she'd actually be saving money by spending it, but it didn't make any sense to her.

"Look," he finally said. He waved a newspaper under her nose. "They got a sale at Sears. These are good coats. They're giving thirty percent off every winter coat in stock, damn it."

Mrs. Woody turned her head away and looked out the window. She didn't like that language he'd picked up, and he knew it.

He softened his tone. "You deserve something nice for a change," he said. He looked at her with sincere eyes. "God, if I had the money, I'd get you one of these coats in a minute."

"I don't want you getting me anything," she snapped.

He thought a minute. "Well, I can tell you this much," he said. "That coat of yours is out of fashion."

"Fashion?" she shot back at him. "You think I give a hoot about fashion when all I ever go to is the cemetery and the grocery store?"

He got up and crossed the room, stumbling against a stack of newspapers she was saving, and fingered the old coat. "This thing won't keep the cold out, that's for sure. And look here, strings hanging, the lining coming out. People will think you're some kind of loony bird."

She lay her hands on the table and looked away from him. "Well maybe I just am."

Since Roy had gone away to business college things had gotten worse between them, not that they'd been that good to begin with. He'd come back more disrespectful and full of ideas, too, none of which was worth two cents. The latest and worst idea was that he was going to marry that trashy girl.

The boy seemed to grow wild after his father died, and Candy was part of that wildness. Then, too, it had taken him an extra year to get his two-year degree. But at least he'd come back home and got himself a job, at Agway, working in the office. And at least he was thinking of her, even if she believed he had something up his sleeve. Maybe he was trying to tell her he wanted to mend things between them. Maybe he'd even come to his senses about that girl.

She almost smiled, picturing herself in a new coat.

"Show me that newspaper, then," she said to him at last.

"Well good God," he said. "It's about time." He got up from the table and hurried around to her side, upsetting her collection of Styrofoam egg cartons, and crashing his foot into a broken birdcage someone had given her. He rattled the newspaper in her face and pointed to the Sears ad and the half dozen coat styles she could choose from.

"I'm only looking," she said. "I'm not buying anything."

Roy drummed his fingers on the hood of his car while he eyed the house, waiting for his mother. The house was falling apart and the lawn hadn't been mowed since August. Now the leaves had started to fall and were beginning to cover the grass. They'd stay that way, too, until the wind blew them away.

Mrs. Woody appeared on the porch, holding a large black pocketbook and a sweater. She threw scraps down for the few chickens she insisted on keeping and watched them scratch through the fallen leaves covering the driveway. She frowned at Roy. "You don't want to take my car?"

For answer, he got in and started his engine.

The exhaust fumes from Roy's car made her dizzy, and she couldn't hear herself think over the sound of the muffler. The car had never run right, either, but he'd bought it just the same, before he went to college, because everybody was always telling him how great slant six engines were, whatever that meant.

"I hope you're not planning to stay long," Mrs. Woody said as she shuffled herself into the front seat. "My TV show's on at eight-thirty." She had to shut the car door twice before it would stay closed. A furry skunk tail hung from the rearview mirror and she bumped it with her head and sent it swinging. "This darn thing," she said, batting at the tail until Roy took it down.

"Well all right, now," he said as he pulled out of the driveway. "Let's get this show on the road."

"If I don't see anything, we're coming right back," she told him. She unclasped the pocketbook and checked inside for the envelope with her money.

Roy figured that once he got her inside the store he could talk her into at least taking a peek at the washing machines. Since hers had broken down she'd started washing her things out by hand. "What else do I have to do with my time?" she'd asked. He had to take his own and Candy's clothes to the laundromat in town.

Roy also wanted to check out the wedge deck radio speakers on sale in the automotive department. And Candy wanted him to look at the ninety-nine-dollar microwave ovens. "You make sure your mother goes with you to look," she'd told him. "She's got to get us some kind of wedding present. At least make her buy something we can use."

"We're only looking for a coat," he told her.

"Make her look at them is all," Candy said. "I always wanted a microwave oven."

Mrs. Woody was fiddling with the vent window. "Can't you do something about that exhaust?" she said. "It's *awful.*"

Just outside the city, Roy swung onto the expressway. "We're almost there," he told her.

"If I live that long," she answered through the handkerchief she held over her nose. "Why are you going this way? You know I hate the expressway."

"You said you wanted this to be a fast trip."

"I said short, not fast."

A terrible screaming noise started up from the engine.

"What in God's name?" Mrs. Woody cried.

Roy took his foot from the gas and felt the control knobs on the dashboard. He leaned forward to listen while he steered the car.

"What *is* it?" she asked him. "Is it the engine?" She clutched the purse in her lap.

"I don't know what it is." He pulled the car onto the shoulder and turned off the engine. "I hope it's not the water pump," he said.

"Well, this is a *fine* thing."

Roy got out and raised the hood while his mother sat hugging her purse. She watched him move from one side of the car to the other, poking under the hood. When he went around back and opened the trunk, she got out.

"What is it?" she asked.

"Thank God I had some oil in the trunk," he said. "There's barely a drop left in the engine."

"Well, what kind of fool drives with no oil?" she said.

He opened the cans with his jackknife and poured two quarts in. "I hope to hell that's all it was," he said. He got back in the car and started it. The engine screamed, and Mrs. Woody jumped back, raising a hand to her face.

"It's going to explode," she shouted to him. "It's smoking."

Roy cut the engine and came around front. "Christ Almighty," he said to his mother. He looked under the hood. He felt around inside the engine, and when his hand touched a shiny belt, he pulled back. "It's the goddamn belt burning up," he said.

"Can you fix it?" Mrs. Woody asked.

"Maybe I can get that belt off," he said. He looked

around at what little traffic chugged up and down the expressway. He touched the belt again, trying to figure out what it was attached to and how to take it off.

"Is there a gas station anywhere?" his mother asked.

"Now how the hell would I know?" Roy answered.

"I wish you'd stop that," she told him.

"Oh for Christ's sakes," he said. He went for a screwdriver and pried at the belt for a little while. He started the engine again, and it screamed and smoked. Mrs. Woody backed away and ducked her head so she wouldn't get hit in the face by flying debris when the whole thing blew.

He shut the engine and sat with his hand to his forehead for a minute. He started the car again, and the same thing happened.

"I knew something like this was going to happen," Mrs. Woody said to him when he came back around to the front of the car. "And you ask me why I never go anywhere."

Roy stared at the smoke curling from the engine. He squinted his eyes and looked out across the expressway to see where they were.

"Now what?" she asked him. "You couldn't even break down on a road we know. No, it had to be here, nowhere."

He shook his head, looking down the expressway.

"Is there anybody you can call?" she asked.

"Nobody that's home."

"Well, I certainly don't know anybody," she told him.

"I'll have to drive it to a gas station," he said.

"You can't drive like this. It'll blow up."

"It's only the goddamn *belt*," he told her.

"Well I'm not riding in this car," she said. "I'm staying here until you do something that makes sense."

"Look," he said, "the bus station's down that street."
He pointed across the lanes. There was an exit a few feet
up the expressway, on the other side. "You can wait in the
bus station for me. I'll drive you that far."

"You walk right over there and call a tow truck, that's
what you can do."

"I'm not calling no tow truck," he told her. "I can
drive as far as a gas station, and it won't cost me nothing
to do it."

"You're going to ruin your car—what's left of it.
That's what it'll cost you."

"I'm telling you the damn car won't blow up," he
shouted. "Now get inside so we can get the hell out of
here."

If they hadn't been out in public, she would have
slapped his face. She turned her back to him and folded her
arms across her chest. She felt something rise up in her—
some old forgotten feeling. Sometimes she wondered why
she'd ever bothered to have a child.

"Well, I'm going," he said. His voice shook a little
from having yelled at her, and she was glad.

"You going to just stand here on the side of the road?"
he said. "Or what?"

When she wouldn't answer, he became almost apolo-
getic. "I'll *walk* you over, all right? And then come back
here and drive the car by myself to a gas station."

She turned on him. "And then what? What am I
supposed to do waiting in some smelly bus station with you
God-knows-where with a car that doesn't run?"

"I'll come get you as soon as I fix the car."

She looked across the expressway, her face rigid. "I
don't see any bus station."

He pointed. "I'll go with you. They got chairs to sit
in and probably a coffee machine."

"Coffee?" she spat. "What do I want with coffee?"

When she turned on him like that he felt like a little boy again. As much as he liked to think she was ridiculous beyond hope, the worst thing in the world he could imagine was losing her. "Well you can't walk over there alone," he told her. "It's too dangerous at night."

"Dangerous?" she yelled. "I'll tell you what's dangerous. Listening to you. That's how I got here in the first place. You're not walking me anywhere."

He took a step back, like he'd been struck. After a while he fumbled in his pockets. "At least take this," he said, handing her some change. "If you get thirsty, or if they got those pay toilets."

She gave him a vicious look. She pulled her sweater on and clutched the purse to her body. "Look at that," she said, nodding to the pink color in the sky. "It's already getting dark. I don't know how I get into these things with you. I don't know what I did that you had to turn out this way."

She turned to go, and he started after her. "Don't you dare follow me," she told him. "Don't you dare come anywhere near me until you've got that car fixed."

He shoved the change back in his pocket and watched her go. He waited until she got across to the other side and was headed for the exit. Then he started the engine and did a U-turn. When he neared her, the car smoking and screeching, he pointed to show her the direction she should go, then raised his hand to wave good-bye. She put her hands to her ears and turned away from him.

Once the sound of his car died away, her head began to clear. She had a little moment of panic when she wished she had agreed to ride with him, exploding engine and all.

She lurched over the uneven grass, with all its hidden bumps and holes, to get to the sidewalk, and began sweating, as cool as the air was. Only a few cars passed by, but nobody seemed to take notice of her. Still, she was embarrassed to think what she must look like. Once she reached the sidewalk she moved more easily, but she still had to watch out to step around smashed beer cans and a hubcap and a pile of broken glass.

Bus station, he'd said. But there wasn't any bus station, none that she could see anyway. There wasn't anything except empty buildings: a giant tire warehouse, a boarded-up used furniture store. She reached what she'd thought was the main street, but found it full of the same thing: nothing.

When Roy was away it had been easier to pull the blinds on some facts of her life. Now that he was back, the old gnawing, uneasy feeling was back, too: that he was her son, and that she'd had something to do with the way he turned out.

She started in the other direction. Trash blew along the gutters. The cool, damp air smelled of dirt and crumbling brick. Only a couple cars passed. She shivered as she realized she was in the kind of place where things happened to people.

She stopped at the corner. Up ahead was an abandoned gas station and a used car lot. She looked at the street sign, but it meant nothing to her. All she knew was the boulevard where the department stores were, and the highway they usually took into the city. Roy hadn't told her what street the bus station was on, and she had a terrible thought: Maybe this was the wrong exit altogether.

She went back the way she'd come. Maybe there'd be a phone booth down the other block. She passed a dented garbage can filled to the brim with broken wood slats and plaster. Even the trash here was useless.

The most unusual thing she had ever found thrown away was a ten-by-fourteen gold-framed picture of Jesus, his throbbing heart pierced by an arrow, with little flames leaping up from it. Someone had put it out for spring cleanup, and she'd taken it. The picture stood upright on its own, and in back was a small electric light bulb. When you plugged the picture in, Jesus lit up, and that red heart seemed to pulse and bleed before your eyes, while the flames flickered around it. Sometimes she'd take it from the shelf in her closet and set it on her dresser. She'd plug it in, turn off all the lights, then switch the picture on, and it would make her go still, as if the light of the picture were sucking every difficult thing right out of her.

Not that she had much to do with Jesus anymore. She'd decided a long time ago that if she was anything, it would probably be a Unitarian, since they never mentioned God. Just the same, she could use something to calm her about now.

The sun was going down and it was getting cooler. She pulled the sweater around her and buttoned all the buttons. Two men stood outside a bar up ahead. They stopped talking and looked at her. "Hey, Grandma," one of them called. "I'm all yours," and he laughed. A shock of fear and shame went through her, and she turned and walked away fast. She listened to hear if they were following, but only heard them laughing back near the doorway.

She was afraid, in a way she had never been before. All her life she had been so careful to always be prepared. And here she was, danger everywhere. It was as if she had been sleeping nicely in her fresh, comfortable bed and someone—something—had whisked her up and dropped her here, of all places. But why? What had she done?

She came to the corner and stopped. When she finally got the courage to look behind her, she saw a woman approaching, from down past the bar. She was a small black woman, and she wore a large, bright yellow knit hat. She walked so slowly that she hardly seemed to be moving. But eventually she reached the men, who didn't even give her a glance, and kept coming.

Mrs. Woody looked up the other street, then at her wrist, pretending she was wearing a watch and was waiting for someone. Every once in a while, though, she'd glance back to check the woman's progress, and was relieved each time she saw the yellow hat bobbing closer.

When the woman reached Mrs. Woody she slowed down, if it was possible to go any slower and still be moving. She turned her head to Mrs. Woody without looking at her, and nodded as she continued her slow walk to the corner.

"How are you?" Mrs. Woody blurted. What she meant to say was "Stop! Help! Something awful has happened to me."

The woman came to a standstill. She smiled, looking up at the buildings. "Oh, I'm pretty good," she said.

Everything about her was slow: her speech, her walk, her movements. "It's cold," she said, looking up at the buildings. She shook her head. "Mm-mm. Lord, it's cold."

It was chilly, yes, but not cold. She was dressed in a pale lavender coat, the color almost faded out of it. She clutched a crumpled Rexall Drugstore bag to her breast. And that yellow hat! It was obviously hand-knit, of thick, bulky yarn, an original all right, something halfway between an oversized tam and a sawed-off bakers' hat. The woman had pulled it way down over her ears, in a way that made her look ridiculous, with her small nose and fine cheekbones poking out from under all those coils of thick yellow yarn. She looked like some kind of exotic bird—or one of those people from a foreign country who wrap their heads in cloth. Who would wear such a thing out in public?

"It *is* getting a little cold, isn't it?" Mrs. Woody said politely.

The woman laughed, looking up the street. "Everything getting higher, too," she said.

Mrs. Woody glanced at the buildings to see what she meant.

"Can't buy nothing no more," the woman said.

"Well, that's the truth," Mrs. Woody answered, seeing her opening. "Why, right this minute I'm supposed to be in Sears buying a coat I don't even want and can't afford. It was my son's foolish idea. And his car broke down and he left me here. He told me to wait in the bus station, but there's no station in sight. I've looked all over for it. Thank goodness you came along—" She was out of breath. She looked at the woman, full of hope.

"Ha!" the woman said, startling Mrs. Woody. "You go to the store and spend all your money, and it don't hardly even put nothing in the bag. Hardly worth to carry it home."

"That's right," Mrs. Woody said, a little confused. She waited, but the woman said nothing more. "I have to find the bus station," Mrs. Woody said at last. "My son—"

"Mm-mm," the woman said, glancing her way again without meeting her eyes. "An' it's so *cold.*"

"Yes, it's cold, all right," Mrs. Woody said, disheartened. "It's cold, and things are getting higher."

The woman laughed, as if this was the funniest thing she had ever heard in her life. She stood slowly nodding her head at the sidewalk, looking pleased. "Now you're saying something," she told Mrs. Woody.

Mrs. Woody stared at her. What if Roy had called the bus station looking for her? What if he'd fixed the car and was there right now, looking for her? He'd just figure she'd found someone to drive her home, and he'd go home, too, and then what?

A car went by, an old junk driven by a middle-aged man with tangled hair and a mustache.

"Lots of people out tonight," the woman said. "Going places fast." She chuckled to herself.

The street was deserted. Most of the streetlights had come on, even though it wasn't dark yet. Down in the next block, the bar's sign glowed red in the window, casting an eerie light on the two men. They stood hunched together with their hands in their pockets and nudged each other as they talked. Mrs. Woody had the strange feeling that they were planning something that involved her.

She turned to the woman, who stood clutching her paper bag and nodding into space. "My, that's a beautiful hat," she blurted.

The woman looked at Mrs. Woody for the first time. Her eyes were like little brown marbles lying under pools of water. "A *friend* give me this hat," she said, beaming.

The woman's smile made the skin stretch across her cheeks in a way that reminded Mrs. Woody of an antique lamp she'd once seen, the shade made of heavy, semiopaque paper that barely let any light through. The force of the smile had parted the woman's lips, too, and a piece of gold glinted at Mrs. Woody from her front tooth.

"My God," Mrs. Woody gasped.

The woman nodded. She looked up and down the street. "I didn't know it was so cold out," she said, and she shivered. "I came out this morning to feed the birds. Lord, it was cold then. An' it's cold now."

Feed the birds? Mrs. Woody could just see it: the woman hobbling along the deserted street with a cellophane bread bag full of crusts, a flock of pigeons swooping and cooing around her.

"I have to find a telephone!" Mrs. Woody shouted. "I have to leave a message for my son."

"Uh-huh," the woman said. "I know."

"My son's going to try to find me," Mrs. Woody cried, "and I won't be there."

The woman shook her head, smiling, with an understanding look. "I know it," she said. "Yes I do."

The two men down at the bar laughed and looked their way. One began to walk toward them, but the other laid his hand on the man's arm. He said something and the man made low growling sounds that started them both snickering.

"For God's sakes," Mrs. Woody cried. "Do you know where there's a telephone?"

The woman seemed to come to attention. She gathered herself together, rustling her paper bag, and looked away from Mrs. Woody.

"One's in my building," she said. "For sure."

It seemed to Mrs. Woody that a long time passed before she was able to speak. "Your building?" she said. "Where you live?"

And right then and there a new vision opened before her. She gazed up at the crumbling, destitute buildings. It had never occurred to her to think of stepping inside one of them.

"Up the street," the woman said. "Right where we headed."

We, Mrs. Woody thought. A little shiver ran through her. "Do you think—?" she said. "Would it be all right—?"

"It cost a quarter," the woman said.

Mrs. Woody breathed a sigh of relief. Of course she would pay for the call. Of course. There wasn't anything wrong with that.

She looked expectantly at the woman, waiting for her to say something more. But the woman stood smiling up at the buildings, as if their conversation about the phone had not even taken place.

But then Mrs. Woody realized that the woman's arms and legs were getting into motion. Without a sound she had stepped off the curb and started across the street. Mrs. Woody followed, uncertain of what had gone on between them, uncertain that she was even meant to follow.

She walked as if in a dream, aware only of the occasional sound of glass crunching under her feet, and the cold smell of soot in the air, not knowing where she was going, but hoping it was somewhere.

The front door of the building was stuck. The woman had to push against it with her shoulder to get it open. And there they were, inside. A steep flight of stairs rose before them, and Mrs. Woody looked up into the darkness where they disappeared. A bare light bulb hung above them, suspended from the longest frayed cord she had ever seen. It barely cast enough light for them to see each other.

The woman struggled to shut the door, and now Mrs. Woody made out the hallway with its line of closed doors. Behind the door they'd just entered sat a box of junk. Old clothes, a tattered lampshade, a broken toy truck, and ripped magazines spilled from the box. Propped on top of everything, and leaning against the wall, stood a plastic flamingo with part of one wing missing. It looked like the kind of thing people might stick on their front lawns—if they had front lawns.

"Now I climb the mountaintop," the woman said. She had already shuffled her way up a few steps.

Mrs. Woody glanced up at her, then back at the door. When she caught sight of the box again, with its flamingo perched on top, something came over her. The tips of her fingers barely touched the railing, and she took careful little breaths as she followed the woman. The air was cool and filled with a crazy mixture of smells: cigar and cigarette smoke, a hodgepodge of cooked food, enamel paint, and something else, sour, like stale wine or vomit.

The smells frightened her. But when she looked back down the stairs at the door she thought of one thing: the other side of it. At least here she knew there was a telephone. And those who lived in this building were, after all, only people, she told herself (although she hadn't seen any of them and was afraid to imagine what they looked like). Harmless people, with their own lives to worry about. In the dim light below, the flamingo appeared almost alive. It perched in its corner and seemed to be telling her, "Go, find your telephone. No harm will come to you." She turned and followed the woman to the top of the stairs.

The second floor was in worse condition than the first. Plaster fell from the walls, and the numbers on some of the doors were missing. Behind one door, with its number 5 dangling upside down, a baby cried. Muffled TV sounds came from another apartment and, from somewhere, the sound of people arguing.

All her life Mrs. Woody had found herself drawn to the very things she swore to avoid. There was no love in the world, only terror—she'd figured out that much a long time ago. When the terror got too much, you clutched at whatever was in front of you and held on for dear life. Like she'd done with Roy's father, and later with Roy himself. She knew her son was shiftless, with a cold stone for a heart, and that she was nothing but a piece of baggage to him, something to cash in. There was nothing she could do to change any of it.

The woman wasn't going anywhere. Maybe she was entirely crazy. Maybe she didn't even live in the building, Mrs. Woody thought. She looked like she planned to walk right into the wall ahead of her.

Mrs. Woody determined that she would very clearly, once and for all, ask for—demand—directions to the bus station, and then get out of there. She passed a door that stood open a crack, and a brown child dressed only in underpants peered out. Mrs. Woody stopped and stared at him. She moved closer to him and as she did an arm reached for the child and pulled him inside. The door shut in her face, and a bolt slid into place.

The old woman stopped at the last door. She stood fumbling through a small change purse. "There," she said, looking up at the door.

Mrs. Woody reached her. "What?" she said at last, looking at the door, too. "What's there?"

The woman pulled a piece of string from her change purse. At the end dangled a key. She gave Mrs. Woody a sidelong glance, as if she couldn't figure her out. "The telephone," she said. "What you think we been talking about?"

Mrs. Woody was confused. And then she saw, just a few feet away, at the very end of the hall, a pay phone.

"Well, God in heaven," she said. She turned to the

phone, and as she did, she heard a click. She looked back in time to see the woman disappear through the door, the fastest move she'd made all night.

Her quarter would not go in the slot. She tried dimes and nickels, but every slot was jammed with slugs. She dialed anyway, and nothing happened. She kept dialing 0, then slamming the receiver up and down, then shouting into it, but the phone was dead.

Mrs. Woody knocked on the woman's door. "Let me in," she called. When the woman didn't answer, she called louder, "Open up. Please. Open up!" But there was no answer.

She leaned against the door, trying to think. If she made too much noise, people would come out to see what the commotion was, and there was no telling what they would do to her. There was nothing left for her to do but go back the way she'd come. Hopefully the men outside the bar would be gone by now. She would go as fast as she could in the other direction and hope to heaven she didn't run into any other characters. If worse came to worse, she decided, she would run out into the middle of the street and scream at the top of her lungs for the police.

The door gave, and Mrs. Woody almost lost her footing. The woman peeked at her through the cracked door. She still wore the yellow hat, but had taken off the coat. Her dress hung on her as if there was nothing more than a wire coat hanger underneath it. Great splotches of pink flowers and green ivy grew up the dress, reaching for that yellow hat.

"The phone's jammed," Mrs. Woody cried. "It's jammed full of slugs." The funniest smell wafted out the door. It was pungent, like eucalyptus.

The woman looked at her with those watery eyes and

slowly nodded her head. But then something seemed to sweep over her face, a look of pity or compassion, as if she was finally understanding what Mrs. Woody had been trying to tell her all night. And now Mrs. Woody felt relief, at last, at having gotten through to her.

"You in a mess, ain't you?" the woman said.

She pulled the door open. Mrs. Woody saw a flickering black and white TV with a plastic flower arrangement sitting on top of it. Curled photographs that all looked vaguely familiar were taped to the wall above the overstuffed sofa. She stood trying to figure out if the woman meant for her to come inside.

From out of nowhere a man appeared and stood next to the woman. He was a muscular black man, mean-looking, with a closely shaved head and wearing a dingy undershirt and blue jeans. Mrs. Woody took a step back. The man looked hard at her, as if he would bellow an insult at her for interrupting them. She shook her head helplessly, ready to explain and make her exit, when he thrust the crumpled drugstore bag the old woman had been carrying in her face, and she jumped.

She opened her hands to him to show she didn't understand what he meant and that she'd meant no harm. He did not back down. He held the bag in front of her eyes as if to remind her of something awful she'd done.

"Please . . . what is it?" she asked, desperate to straighten out the misunderstanding and leave.

He watched her face closely. There was something strange about him.

The woman took the bag from the man. "That's all right," she told him. "I get you some now."

She fumbled to open the bag, and finally took a roll of candies from it.

"This is my boy, Axel," the woman told Mrs. Woody.

When he heard his name, the man gave Mrs. Woody a wide, open-mouthed grin that showed teeth and bright pink gums. She felt her own mouth open, as if to shriek, but nothing came out.

The man turned his eyes back on the woman as she unwrapped a piece for him. Mrs. Woody tried to back away, but nothing worked on her.

When the woman handed the man the candy he popped it into his grinning mouth. Then he moved forward suddenly and gave the old lady a slobbering kiss, right under the yellow hat.

Mrs. Woody ran. She reached the stairs and nearly fell as she hurried down them sideways, both hands on the one railing. The door was stuck, and she had to yank on the knob until it finally gave. The sudden movement threw her off-balance, but she caught the wall with her arm and kept herself from falling. When her fingers brushed against the plastic flamingo in the box of junk, she took hold of it and ran out of the building.

She headed toward the boarded-up gas station at the corner, even though she'd been afraid to go that far earlier. She put her hand to her heart, feeling for the palpitations, afraid that she would drop dead right then and there. Just let me make it to the bus station, she thought, and I'll gladly die, if it has to be. But not here on the street. She made herself slow down, so as not to agitate things.

It was nearly dark out. But as she glanced across the empty car lot, she saw a few streaks of red and purple light in the sky. The sight made her stop, in spite of her palpitating heart. Because of the way the land sloped, the city seemed to fall away, and she could see the dark shapes of hills, far in the distance. She was struck by it all: to be standing in the middle of a dirty, torn-up city, lost and terrified, yet able to see clear outside into the forgotten hills, the farmland, maybe even her home, too, out there somewhere. If she had a home. She felt like a gypsy who owned only the clothes on her back and what few things she carried. It seemed that every little thing she cared for had been wrenched right out of her.

She wrapped her arms more tightly around herself and moved on, the pink flamingo and purse clutched awkwardly in front of her, the broken glass and debris crunching under her shoes.

She reached the corner and there it was, right down the street. The bus station was small, but well lighted. If she had gone just a little farther in the first place she would have seen it and wouldn't have been terrorized all night.

There were people inside the bus station. She could see them through the plate glass window. Outside, a bus rumbled, sending puffs of smoke out its exhaust.

As she reached the doors, the dangers of the night seemed to disappear for a moment, and she almost felt a little exhilarated at all she had been through. She pulled the door and it yielded. She tucked the flamingo under her arm and went in.

Here and there a head turned, then went back to its magazine or newspaper. The people sat scattered in molded plastic seats, their bags and bundles on the floor next to them as they waited to be taken places, and her moment of exhilaration passed.

Mrs. Woody took a seat to collect herself. She tried not to think about what had happened to her, but the black woman's face and her son's grinning mouth kept looming in front of her, as if she were having a nightmare right there with her eyes opened. She looked at the posters on the wall of places people could visit and blinked her eyes. It was hard to believe she'd actually gone inside the black woman's building. In fact, Mrs. Woody found it hard to believe she was sitting alone right now in a cold, dirty bus station in the middle of nowhere when she was supposed to be home in front of her TV, watching people sing and waltz and laugh with each other.

She felt that she was missing something, but she couldn't put her finger on what it was. She checked her purse, the money, the sweater. Everything was there.

The flamingo stood propped against the side of her chair, pale and broken in the fluorescent light. When Roy saw it he would have a fit, calling her a junk collector, and her house a trash heap. They'd start right in fighting where they'd left off. Maybe she *was* a junk collector. But at least the junk was hers. At least she had something. Mrs. Woody looked out at the few passengers, to see if they were noticing anything odd about her. But no one was looking her way.

She closed her eyes and shook her head, as if she could shake all the unpleasant feelings right out of her. But instead of going away, everything came clear: Roy and Candy happy together, after her for whatever they could get; and Mrs. Woody alone in her house, knowing what she'd suspected all along—that she'd always be able to hold on a little bit longer in this awful world, no matter how bad things got.

RUDE
AWAKENING

Hannah and her father understood each other. There were times when they had to get away from the noise and commotion of family life. They'd go for rides in the hills, then, to look out over planted fields, or to assess the quality of so-and-so's cows; or else they'd just drive along, keeping their eyes sharp for deer or pheasants or red-tailed hawks. He'd take her in the pickup when he went to make a grain deal, or when he drove to the mill for lumber, or to Agway for seed. When one of the men made a comment about his little helper, he'd wink at her, then shove his hands deep into his pockets and rattle the change, as if he was embarrassed.

Hannah's mother went along with it all. She had other things to worry about. She'd married late in life, her babies had come one after the other, and in between babies she worked at the upholstery factory. She liked to warn her children that she was on the verge of a nervous breakdown and that they were the cause of it.

She would eye Hannah now and then, though, and complain that she didn't know what would happen when she got older and still preferred working in the barn to helping out in the house. And now that it was time for Hannah's First Communion, the worst battle of all was on between them. "I always thought our family would meet again in heaven after we died," her mother told her. "I never dreamed my own daughter wouldn't be there with us."

"If the boys can wear white pants and a jacket, so can I," Hannah argued one last time. "If you tell the nuns it's okay, they'll let me." She turned to her father. "Right, Daddy?"

"Jesus," her father mumbled. "I don't know." He shook his head. "I don't know about that." He rattled the change in his pocket and walked out of the room.

She'd always worn pants, even to school, although the teachers were starting to send notes home to her mother about it. Her father was the one who always said clothes didn't matter and people should wear whatever they were comfortable in. And now he wasn't even sticking up for her.

Of course, she'd known all along that the white or- gandy and lace dress was coming, but she believed she would somehow be saved from her fate. At the last minute she would become deathly ill and be rushed by ambulance to the hospital. Or else the bomb would finally drop and the family would have to leave everything behind and scramble for the fallout shelter. And then she wouldn't be able to wear the radioactive dress.

Hannah waited until the very last minute before she put the dress on. She would not stand still to let her mother adjust the belt or collar, nor would she let her brush her tangled hair or put the starched veil on her head. For emphasis, she flung the miraculous medal outside the blouse of the dress, where it did not belong, and it dangled off one shoulder.

Her mother shook her head. "I just wish you could see what you look like."

"I don't care," Hannah answered.

"Someday you'll care," her mother told her. That was one of her favorite expressions. "Someday you'll have a batch of kids just as bad as you, then you'll care. I hope you have a dozen of them."

Katie stuck her tongue out at her sister, and Hannah knew she would have to slap her for it later.

Then the baby started in. Their mother had put her in the crib to keep her out of trouble while the others got dressed. The baby hated the crib because she knew she was too big for it. She tried to climb out, but her leg stuck between the bars, and now she hung head down over the railing, screaming.

Their mother ran to rescue her, then dressed her for church while Katie—mother's little darling—looked after their brother. He was crying because his church shoes were too small and pinched his feet.

Their father paced through the house, swearing to himself. Finally, he went out back to walk in his corn lot until the family was ready.

Hannah stomped outside behind him, to wait on the

porch. She brushed off the top step and sat down, the dress billowing in her lap. The skirt was made of layers of slips and netting that swelled around her and that scratched and rustled whenever she moved. When she sat, she had to press her hands against the material in her lap to keep it from flying up and baring her legs.

From where she sat, she could see her father walking along the freshly plowed field, dressed in his blue suit. Every now and then he'd bend to pluck a weed or stone from the earth and toss it aside. Hannah wanted to be out there in the field with him, dressed in her overalls and flannel shirt, helping him like she always did, and a new flurry of rage went through her.

The problem with First Communion wasn't just the dress. She felt she was being forced to give in to all the threats and accusations she'd ever heard about her needing to "straighten out" and become a "proper girl"—something she already thought she was—if she wanted to get through life. Going through with the ceremony meant she agreed with them: that she must have been born with something terribly wrong.

Her mother came on to the porch with the other three and called for Hannah's father. Hannah waited for them near the car, feeling trapped in the dress, as if she were a stick that had been skewered through the center of a great white paper flower. Before they got in the car, Hannah's father looked at her. It was the first time he had seen her in her full Communion outfit, and he shook his head.

"Aren't you something?" he said. "We can't put you to work in the barn dressed like that." He chuckled to himself as he got in the driver's seat.

Her face burned. She knew he meant to say she was hideous, which she didn't need to be reminded of. It was bad enough having everyone else after her, but to hear it from him, too, was too much. There were times in her life when she had played with the idea of murdering her mother and sister. She now added her father to the list.

As they drove off, she crumpled the veil in her hands, hoping she would be able to ruin it before they got to church.

The baby blabbered to herself in the front seat. Katie and Anthony gabbed on about the party their grandmother was having for Hannah after Mass. They were excited about everything—the big dinner, the presents Hannah would get, the cousins they'd see. The happier they sounded, the angrier she became.

"Shut up," she told them.

"Don't have to," Katie said. Then she piped out for their mother to hear, "She's wadding her veil."

"Don't you dare," her mother told her.

"I am not," Hannah said. She reached across Anthony and pinched Katie's arm. Katie let out a scream as if something had been broken on her.

"Judas Priest," their father shouted.

"This is supposed to be a holy time," her mother said from the front seat. "Remember, you went to confession yesterday."

Hannah turned her face to the window. She was still shaken from having spoken her sins out loud to a stranger. Worse, she was afraid she had sinned further by being so vague with him: She had had "bad thoughts" three times, she'd told him. She had talked back to her parents four times, disobeyed them twice, used bad words three times. *She* knew what she had done. She was afraid the priest knew, too. And now she was certain he would recognize her in church this morning.

"Before you go up for Communion," her mother told her, "you'd just better say a prayer and ask God to forgive you again." She pronounced it "Gawd."

"So there," Katie said. Hannah took another swing at her, but she pulled back.

In truth, Hannah's heart was tortured. The thought of hell terrified her, yet she could not stop sinning. She knew her mother was right: She would have to confess again. But she didn't know if it was safe to do it herself, in private, or if they would have to call the priest for a special hearing in order to make it work, and the thought of facing him again made her shudder. She couldn't let on to her family, though, that she had any doubts or was afraid. And of course she couldn't let her mother think she was right.

During the ride to church, Hannah's father had said nothing more than "Judas Priest" to the bickering and "Yes" when their mother had asked if he'd remembered the church envelopes. Hannah knew he was miserable. He couldn't stand to dress up any more than she could, he hated church and family get-togethers, and he hated his children's fights. He began to whistle, which is what he did whenever he was nervous or annoyed. That is, he tried to whistle. Since he'd lost most of his teeth, he couldn't make a decent sound, but that didn't stop him from trying.

His pitiful attempt made Hannah ashamed that she'd thought of murdering him—and afraid, too, that she'd have to confess it. "Daddy," she told her father, "as soon as church is over I'm going to help you plant the corn."

"You're going to Grandma's with the rest of us," her mother snapped. "Don't go getting any of your funny ideas now."

"I'm going with Daddy," Hannah insisted.

"Fine," her mother said. "Because he's coming with

us." She looked at him as she said this, but he didn't say anything back.

He whistled and tapped the steering wheel with his fingers, keeping his eyes straight ahead as he drove.

The most awful thing in Hannah's life was about to happen, and there was nothing she could do to stop it. As they pulled into the church parking lot, she tucked the miraculous medal back inside the dress.

"I've brought the hairbrush," her mother announced. "Now let me fix that hair of yours before anybody sees you."

Hannah drew back as her mother turned to face her, and the gesture pushed her mother over the edge. "You think the world was made just to suit you, don't you?" she exploded. She turned farther in her seat, and pointed the hairbrush at the girl.

"Goddamn Almighty," their father grumbled.

Katie grinned at Hannah.

Her mother shook the hairbrush in Hannah's face. "You're going to have a rude awakening one of these fine days," she told her. "Then we'll see if you don't change your tune."

Hannah watched the others in the parking lot. They seemed so cheerful, as if nothing terrible was happening to them. She knew that once she got out of the car she would have to act cheerful, too, or else they would learn the awful truth about her: that she was abnormal, after all.

"I can brush my own hair," she told her mother.

"Well," her mother said, relieved. She handed Hannah the brush, and she dragged it through her own hair.

They got out of the car. Not one other family looked like theirs. No one was making a scene. No one else was miserable.

"Don't forget to put your veil on," her mother said. The baby squirmed in her arms, but she wouldn't let her down because of the cars. Katie held Anthony's hand and swung it while he tried to tug away.

Their father stood off to the side, his hands in his pockets, impatiently jingling his change. Something struck Hannah, then, seeing him like that, standing apart with his hands in his pockets. She was his favorite, his helper. Yet he had not spoken one word in her behalf during all her ordeal. She realized what a coward he was, and it stung her.

"We'll be watching for you," Hannah's mother said. Her voice had lost its edge. "Good luck." She clutched the baby and looked down at Hannah, and her eyes filled with tears.

Hannah was afraid her mother was going to start crying, right there in front of everyone, so she backed away. "I'll see you," she mumbled, and she turned and headed for the church hall. The dress made a hideous rustling sound as she walked, and a lump rose in her throat.

The classroom was dark and cold. A few girls huddled together, whispering and giggling. Some of the boys ran up an aisle and then slid across the floor in their new shoes. Hannah stayed by herself, feeling too ugly to speak to anyone.

The nuns seated them for prayers and last-minute instructions. She refused to pray. She refused to listen to a word they were saying. But when she saw one of the nuns scowling at her bare head, she put the veil in place. The headband dug into her scalp, and the lace scratched her ears.

Finally, they filed outdoors and into the church.

On one side of Hannah knelt Juanita Bell with her oily hair and smelling, as usual, like dirty underclothes. Hannah squirmed as far from her as she could without touching the girl on her other side. The girl gave Hannah a look as if to say she understood, then bowed her head to pray. Hannah had seen her on the school playground. She was short and fat, with a Buster Brown haircut, the only other girl who could kick home runs in kickball. Hannah glanced down at the girl's hands and was shocked to see the square fingernails painted with light pink nail polish.

When the Mass started, she adjusted the headband again, to keep it from digging into her. She watched the altar boys kneel and stand and give the priest a cup or book and follow him to one spot, then another. When they knelt, she stared at the scuffed soles of their shoes.

Now that her First Communion had actually started, things weren't as awful as she'd expected—except for the scratchy clothes and the thought of going up in front of everyone and having the priest put the host on her tongue. She was afraid of having the body and blood of Jesus Christ in her mouth. And she worried about having to eat it without chewing, the way her grandfather who didn't have any teeth ate his food.

As the priest droned on in Latin, Hannah looked at the gilt altar crucifix and tried to imagine the eternal damnation her mother was so certain was waiting for her. All she could muster was a gnawing fear at the thought of time everlasting—whether spent burning in hell or singing the glories of God in heaven. She didn't want to belong to God, although she didn't want to belong to Satan, either.

But if she belonged to neither of them, that would mean spending eternity alone, absolutely alone, without her mother and father, without even a stranger. As the thought of it sank in, her stomach did a terrible empty flop inside her.

She decided then, as she had so many times before, that she would be *good*. She would be saved, in spite of everything. She confessed silently right then to all her sins: slapping her sister, trying to ruin the dress and veil, fighting with her mother, plotting the murder of her family. From now on she would do whatever God asked of her. She would stop fighting, and she would become a saint. To prove that she meant it, just in case God was listening, she inched back toward smelly Juanita Bell.

The girls in front of her stood. The nuns were directing them to the altar. She had lost track of everything, and now there was no time to prepare herself. Her row stood up, and she with them.

She walked in a daze, feeling like she'd just waked up and wasn't quite sure where she was going or why. Everyone craned to get a look at them as they marched to the altar. Hannah couldn't see her parents, but she knew that they, too, were straining to pick her out of the crowd.

She took her place at the railing, her palms sweating and pressed together. She wondered if she would feel anything when the host was put in her mouth. She imagined an earthquake or thunder, or at least a shock wave going through your body when God entered. Out of the corner of her eye she saw the priest and altar boy approach, heard the mumbled words repeated. Then the priest stood in front of her. He held the host before her eyes and mouthed the *Corpus domini* while she looked up. His hand was fat and pale, as if it had never seen the sun.

He waited for her, but she was too frightened to move. His plump fingers hovered near her mouth, and she could smell their unnatural cleanliness. He waved the host closer.

Finally, she put her tongue out, as she had been instructed to. The priest put the host on her tongue and moved on.

There was no earthquake. But nothing the nuns had told them prepared Hannah for what was inside her mouth. It was dry and weightless and tasted of cardboard, with a faint flavor of glue.

When they returned to their seats, she knelt and looked around at the others. Girls with surprised and pious expressions moved their jaws and swallowed. She lowered her eyes and tried to move the host with her tongue.

The wafer turned gummy. And then it became stuck to the roof of her mouth. The nuns had told them they shouldn't worry if such a thing happened: They would be able to free it with their tongues. Of course, they were forbidden to touch the consecrated host with their fingers. Only the priest was allowed to do such a thing.

But there was no freeing it. She worked at it; it would not budge. When she saw that all the other mouths were still, she became embarrassed, and decided to leave the wafer alone in hopes that it would dissolve on its own.

As soon as church was over she would tell her mother she was sick and had to go home. She would strip the dress off, throw on her dungarees and shirt, and scramble up to the tree fort she'd been building. She would lie on the platform under the cool branches and forget the awful day.

She made a motion to swallow and realized her mouth had filled with saliva. There was so much and it seemed so awful that she could not swallow it. So the trick became to allow her throat its reflex swallowing motions without letting anything go down. If she could just hold on until Mass was over, she could hurry outside behind the tall hedges and spit out the saliva and swallow the host.

A little pile of crumbs lay on the ledge below the

stained-glass window. Hannah stared hard at it to distract herself, wondering what the crumbs could be. Maybe termites were eating the wood and the church would soon tumble down. Or maybe a mouse had taken one of the dry hosts but couldn't stand the taste either, and had left it.

The Mass finally ended. But then it seemed to take them forever to get outside the church. As soon as she breathed fresh air, she tried to walk faster and headed for the shrubs, but dozens of people milled around, blocking her escape. And then a photographer lined them up on the church steps. Her throat ached. She avoided her classmates for fear they would speak to her and expect an answer, and when she did meet them she grinned or grunted, then quickly turned away.

At last the photographer let them go. Hannah's family found her, and they headed for the car. Hannah dreaded riding all that way with her mouth full of spit. She was afraid, too, that somehow she was committing a mortal sin. Suddenly the thought came to her that by the time she finally was able to get rid of the saliva the host would be dissolved and she'd be spitting it out, too. That would mean she had never really taken her First Communion—and you had to, in order to be able to go to Communion the rest of your life.

"Well," her mother said. It was the one word she used whenever anything good, awful, or otherwise noteworthy happened and she didn't know what else to say. Her face was flushed, as if she was the one who had been through the ordeal.

Hannah's father walked along with his hands in his pockets, jingling his change, now and then making a self-conscious nod to an acquaintance. He began to hum to himself, glad that church was over.

"You looked nice," Hannah's mother said, her color back to normal.

Katie walked ahead, swinging Anthony's arm.

"Aunt Rose came," her mother said. "I didn't even invite her to Grandma's. She gave me an envelope for you." She rummaged in her purse with her one free hand and gave Hannah the white envelope.

They got in the car.

"Well, let's go eat," her father said. "Are you hungry?" he asked Hannah.

She shrugged her shoulders which, of course, he couldn't see.

"Now that wasn't so bad, was it?" her mother said to her as they pulled onto the street.

She didn't answer. She pressed the skirt down into her lap.

Katie wanted to know if she would get her own First Communion dress or if she would have to wear Hannah's.

"We'll see," her mother said.

"I want my own," she said. "I don't want to wear hers."

"My, you're being awfully quiet," Hannah's mother said to her.

"Cat's got her tongue," Katie said. "Good thing."

Hannah turned her face to the open window and carefully inhaled, trying not to choke.

"Let's see Aunt Rose's card," her mother said.

Hannah was sick. She didn't know if she could last the car ride. She opened the envelope and handed the card to her mother.

"Well. A dollar," she said. "You better not forget to tell her thank-you."

Hannah's father told her mother, "Don't think I'm staying all day at this party."

"You don't have to stay all day," she told him.

"I've got to finish putting in the corn, that's all," he said.

"Did I say anything?" she answered.

They were almost there. Her mother asked Hannah if she'd been nervous when she went up for Communion.

"Mm-mm," she said.

"Howcome she's not talking?" Katie asked.

Hannah's mother turned in her seat to look at her.

A queer expression came over her face, and Hannah panicked, thinking her mother could see what had happened.

"Well," she said. "I'll be." She leaned her head to one side and looked at Hannah. Finally she said, "She's so moved by the ceremony she can't speak."

The effect of those words sent something cold through Hannah's heart. "Thank *God,*" her mother's face seemed to say, "something has finally touched you. Something has finally straightened you out."

She turned back and faced the front. "Now let's just see how long this lasts."

When they got to their grandmother's, Katie and Anthony ran ahead to look for their cousins. Her mother lifted the baby out, then let her down and held her hand. She had Hannah's father search back through the front seat for the diaper bag.

"This?" he said, holding it up. She nodded. He swung the bag for the baby, to be funny, and began singing a tune about the "mosquitoes biting tonight." Hannah hung back near the sidewalk, away from them.

"Aren't you coming in?" her mother asked her.

"Um-hmm."

"I should hope so," she said. "This would be a fine

time for you to throw a fit." But then she looked at Hannah with that look again. Her father held the bag still, and his eyes were on Hannah, too, but he seemed to be thinking of something else.

Her mother headed for the house, clutching the baby's hand, and her father followed. He held the door for them, then scraped his shoes on the step—a habit from the farm—and walked in after them.

Hannah went around to the side of the house and looked to make sure there were no cars or people in sight. Then she leaned one hand against her grandmother's elm tree, and she spit everything out.

She had not meant for it to be that way. She had expected all along to swallow the host, just like everyone else, and then be released from the whole affair. But now something new had begun for her, something no one had prepared her for.

She headed for the house, to join the party, where she would be the center of attention and receive gifts for what had happened to her. Tears stung her eyes.

So this was it, she thought. Her parents had handed her over, both of them, willingly, and this is what she got. She was damned, beyond anything anyone could have imagined. They could not see it, and she could not tell them. Tomorrow at Sunday Mass, and other Sundays afterward, she would have to take Communion again as if nothing had happened. She would never be able to confess.

She reached the door and wiped her eyes, the one lost girl in the world. Just let anybody try to say one word to her, she thought, and she'd let them see what a real sinner was like.

LOSING
WILLY
GLEASON

We were used to all kinds of characters in town, not to mention those that lived up in the hills or out in their shacks on the mucklands and came in Friday nights for groceries. But the Gleasons were something else. We used to call them "those idiot Gleasons," and we could always count on them for a good story to keep things interesting. But it was after Sylvia Biddle and Willy Gleason started walking up and down the road pushing a baby carriage, around the same time he took the shotgun to his mother, that those stories began to take on a new life.

From the distance Willy Gleason appeared to be either a sickly child or a crippled old man. In truth, he was thirty years old, scrawny, with tangled black hair and tight, shiny skin. You'd see him alongside one of those farm roads out where he lived, standing off the shoulder, smoking a cigarette, looking down at the dirt, like he was lost in some deep meditation, or else having a spell of some kind. He never came into town, and he never got within fifteen feet of another person if he could help it. So it was hard to believe that he'd found himself a girlfriend. If Willy Gleason was going to fall for a girl, though, Sylvia Biddle would be the natural choice.

She was another one who didn't have too much upstairs. We'd see her down at Coleman's, buying coloring books, most likely for herself, asking the cashier if she had enough money. Sometimes she'd have to put the coloring book back, sometimes another customer'd overhear and chip in a dime or nickel to make up the difference. Sylvia was short, with a rickety body that made her look like her bones had just missed falling into their right place. Atop that body sat a miniature skull, like a shrunken head, with a jutting chin and tiny bright eyes. She lived in town, over in the Beehive apartments, on the road to the dump.

Willy started coming into town, going over to the Beehive for Sylvia. Then the two of them would walk down the road toward the dump, or sometimes in the other direction, toward downtown, he lagging behind just a little bit, she pushing that carriage with a dumb, miserable look, neither one of them speaking a word. And so it was, Willy Gleason came out to join the living.

We were sitting around Rinaldi's hardware store waiting for the mail to go by with our social security checks. You could call Rinaldi's our retirement club, of sorts. He had a card table set up in the back near his baling wire and we'd sit there playing cards, drinking coffee, and shooting the bull. I was the youngest member—I'd only had my gold watch six months.

"Anybody ever seen that baby?" stone-faced Aldin Cleary said, right in the middle of talking about the car accident on the Milestrip. We looked around at each other. "I got my ideas," Aldin said, "that there ain't no baby in that carriage."

"What they got in there?" Grove said. "Antiques from the dump?"

"I got my ideas."

"What ideas?"

"Could be a few things," Aldin said, drawing on that pipe. "Could be something illegal. Maybe drugs, I was thinking."

"When you're a Biddle or a Gleason," Clarky said, "what's drugs going to do for you that ain't already been done?"

Aldin tamped on the pipe and relit it, drawing hard. "Then I was thinking," he said, "well, maybe it's for somebody else, those drugs, and they're just after making money."

"You're crazy," Rinaldi said.

Aldin nodded. "So then I figured, maybe there ain't nothing in that carriage. Maybe they're up to something, going somewhere they ain't supposed to, or else planning to. But even that takes brains."

"Maybe they're walking around trying to figure out what they got to do to put a baby *in* that carriage," Grove said.

"Just the same," Aldin said, "something's not right about it. You be sure to tell me, now, if you ever see them with a baby."

And that's how we got started on the baby carriage

stories. From what I heard, even the school kids were coming up with their own versions. From then on, whenever Willy Gleason and Sylvia Biddle walked anywhere, you could see people nod their heads at each other, or wink, as if to say *they* knew what was going on, which, of course, nobody did.

Just when those stories were really getting good, the sheriff had an early morning call to get out to the Gleason house fast. Willy Gleason had a shotgun and had let loose with it on his mother while she was hanging out clothes. Word was, he'd got her in the legs, but she'd made it to the chicken coop.

Me, Aldin, Grove, and Clarky followed the sheriff out there, part of the volunteer firemen's contingent that goes on almost any call. Willy kept firing at the coop while the old man, already past drunk, hollered at him to stop and at his wife to come out, the boy didn't mean anything by it. The rest of the Gleasons lined up on the porch, swinging their legs over the side, watching the whole thing. When the old man realized he had an audience—us—his voice went sweet and high-pitched, like he was trying to coax a dog out from under the porch. "Come on, Vallina, come on out now, it's all right," he was saying to her, and to his son he was saying, "Be a good boy, Willy, put that gun down, Willy," until what he was saying turned into a singsong that even the old man got tired of, and he finally gave up and sat down on the porch with the kids.

Willy took no notice of anything. He blasted away at the coop like he was shooting at a row of tin cans, stopping only to reload, while the sheriff held his own gun trained on Willy's back. He called to him a couple times, but Willy didn't even turn his head. We were wondering what the sheriff's next move would be, when Willy stopped. He'd run out of shells. He dropped the shotgun on the ground and stood there for a minute. Then he turned and headed for the house, like nothing had happened. We jumped him, and he went down like a rag doll, just collapsed. Sheriff handcuffed him, stood him up, and walked him over to the car, asking, "What the hell's going on? What the hell you trying to do?"

Willy let himself be led over. He kept his head down, looking at his feet, not answering, like he was walking along by himself thinking of something.

While the sheriff pushed Willy Gleason into the car, the four of us went over to the chicken coop for the old lady. We carried her out, one of us on each limb, and even then we could barely lift her, she was that big. Blood had streamed down her legs and filled her shoes. Her rear end bumped along the ground as we carried her, and she moaned all the way, her eyes fluttering.

As we heaved her onto the porch, Clarky shouted to the old man to call the ambulance.

"No phone," he said.

Nobody moved. The family sat there like they were watching a TV show. "Look at her shoes," one of the kids said.

Finally the sheriff radioed for an ambulance. He left Clarky watching Willy Gleason in the car, and he sent a kid in for some towels to stop the bleeding. The kid came back with a filthy army blanket, and we dabbed at the blood with the blanket while she moaned. Then she got quiet and lay there with her eyes closed.

"Shit, she's all right," the old man said. He leaned close to her, watching her face, and said, "Vallina, you all right?"

The ambulance came, and after taking a look at her

legs and feeling for a pulse, they hefted her into the back. "Flesh wounds," the attendant said. "Lots of blood in the legs." He nodded at the closed doors. " 'Specially when you're like that." Then he got in and drove off. The kids dangled their legs over the side of the porch, one of them chewing on a piece of toast. Another girl tried to ride a bicycle with only one training wheel. She was in her underpants, nothing else.

"I think you better come with me," the sheriff told Old Man Gleason. "I got some questions to ask you."

"What you want me for?" he said. "I didn't do nothing. Was my boy, and you got him."

"I'll be asking him plenty, too, don't you worry," he said.

"I got to get my girls off to school," Gleason said. "I can't go nowhere." Never mind he had some older ones there, seventeen, eighteen year olds that could have taken care of things.

They carried on like that for a while, till the sheriff said maybe he'd just arrest the old man, too, if he didn't feel like coming on his own. So he went, cursing all the way to the car, and calling to Willy in the backseat as he got in, "You son of a bitch."

Of course, there was a lot of speculation about what had caused the shooting. Willy himself had a few different versions. At first he said he didn't know the gun was loaded. "It went off," he told the sheriff, which was a crock, because we all saw him reload and fire about five times. Then he said the first shot that hit her was an accident, but when she put up such a fuss about it, he got mad and went after her, which was probably a little closer to the truth. Finally he muttered something about having wanted to shoot her for a long time. "She bothers me," he said.

"You go shooting at everybody who bothers you?" the sheriff asked him. "What're you trying to do, kill your mother?"

Willy shrugged.

"You don't have to stay in that house if you don't like the people who live there."

Willy smoked his cigarette down to his fingers. Then he snuffed it out in his hand, and he held it, looking at his closed fist, and he didn't say anything more.

The sheriff charged him with disturbing the peace, made him spend the night in jail, and fined him ten dollars.

Meanwhile, the old lady was having a fine time in the hospital. When she found out the welfare was going to cover her bill, she convinced them they should take out her gallbladder. She'd been having attacks for some time, she told them. So they ran tests, and only God and the devil know if they found anything, but they took her gallbladder out just the same.

Aldin Cleary was real happy about the way things were turning out. "I told you," he said. "You see now if something else don't start up." He had the idea, he told us, that there was some connection between the shooting and Willy's attachment to the Biddle girl. "Don't know just what yet," he said, "but something."

So it was no surprise when Pete Early, out on his rural delivery route, noticed the Biddle girl near the Gleason property, walking along with the carriage and Willy. First time we'd ever known her to go out that way. They had stopped near the Bowie pond while she munched on a peach and he leaned against a tree about ten feet off and smoked a cigarette. And that's how it went all the time Vallina was laid up in the hospital. We figured the girl was getting ready to move in, since that's the way those Gleasons usually did things, all one big happy family living together.

But when Vallina was discharged from the hospital, after spending a little more than two weeks recovering from her flesh wounds and gallbladder operation, it wasn't Sylvia Biddle who caused her the trouble.

When Vallina got home, Willy stood in the driveway, leaning on the handle of a pickax. He narrowed his eyes and glared at the old lady. No one else was around, even though everybody knew the county nurse was driving Vallina home that day. It was also the day of the VFW's annual fishing derby, with rides and games and a beer tent, so, naturally, that's where they all were. After a few minutes of having Willy eyeball her the old lady called out for her husband who, of course, wasn't there.

"Where is everybody?" the nurse asked him.

When he answered, "Gone," without once taking his eyes off his mother, the nurse said she thought for sure he'd murdered every one of them, and they were next.

"This is my house," the old lady started shouting.

"Who said it ain't?" Willy answered, and he flexed his grip on the handle.

"Don't leave me here," Vallina told the nurse. "The devil's inside him." Then she bent over double, holding her belly and moaning about her operation and how sick she was and how people were out to kill her.

The nurse shoved the old lady back in the car and took off. By the time they reached the sheriff's, Vallina was carrying on steady about the devil inside Willy and how her stitches were ready to bust open.

"Now what the hell you bring her back here for?" the sheriff said. "What am I supposed to do with her?"

"You do what you want," the nurse told him. "I don't

have time for this foolishness. I got things to do." And she got in her car and drove off.

So the sheriff had Vallina hauled back to the hospital for observation since he didn't know what else to do with her.

The sheriff was starting to get the impression that anything he did involving the Gleasons led to a little more trouble than had been there in the first place. Still, he figured he had a job to do, so he set off to get Willy.

Willy sat on the porch, smoking a cigarette and listening to a transistor radio propped beside him. The pickax lay in the driveway.

"I hear we got a problem out here," the sheriff said to him.

Willy pulled a long drag on his cigarette. He kept his head down, looking at something important on the toe of his shoe.

"What the hell you up to?" the sheriff said.

"Nothing," Willy answered.

"What the hell you doing with that thing, then?" He pointed to the pickax.

Willy looked over at it. "Fixing the driveway," he said.

"Look here, Gleason," the sheriff said. "I can get you for aggravated assault. Or would you rather go for attempted murder?"

Willy put the cigarette out in the palm of his hand and held it.

"You save us all a whole lot of trouble," the sheriff told him. "You be off this place in forty-eight hours."

Willy almost looked surprised for a minute. Then he stared the sheriff straight in the eye. "What's that bitch told you?"

"Forty-eight hours, you hear? I'll be back, too." And the sheriff turned to go. That's when Willy said something about somebody getting hurt bad.

"What's that?" sheriff asked him.

"Don't blame me, that's all," Willy told him.

Back in the car, the sheriff started working up to a good rage. He was madder at himself for getting involved than he was at Willy for causing trouble. But must be he was more curious than mad because when he swung by the fishing derby and spotted the old man outside the beer tent, he pulled over and got out. The old man sat on the grass with his legs sprawled, a paper cup in his hand. Some of the Vets were picking up garbage and taking in chairs.

"I just came from seeing your boy Willy," the sheriff told him.

The old man looked up, blinking, like he was just coming out of a coma.

"What's going on between him and your wife?"

"The no-good son of a bitch," Gleason said.

"He's looking to hurt somebody," the sheriff told him.

"*She* done it," the old man said. "It's her fault."

"What's she done?"

"Look at her." He waved his hand as if she was standing right there, which to his drunken eyes she may have been. "Look at her." He crumpled the paper cup. "It's okay if I don't want none of her. I'm a filthy drunk, she says. But if *he* don't. It's her own fault."

"If he don't what?" the sheriff said. "Who?"

"The son of a bitch," Gleason said. "Willy. Who you think I'm talking about?"

When we got the news, we figured either the sheriff had heard wrong or else the old man was too drunk to talk straight. Nonetheless, we saw Vallina Gleason—the whole

Gleason clan for that matter—in a new light. What we couldn't figure out, though, was why Willy was such a son of a bitch in his father's eyes if it was the old lady who was going after him.

"Maybe," Aldin Cleary offered, "the trouble is the boy don't want her and the old man's insulted. You want to figure a Gleason out, you got to think like a Gleason."

"You're just the one to do it, too, ain't you?" Grove said, and Aldin shot him a look that could make a dead horse get up and walk.

Cranky old men, I thought, and I prayed to God retirement didn't do that to me. It made me want to get looking for a job all over again.

"I wonder what other kinds of perversions they do out there," Clarky said. And we thought about it.

Two days later, the sheriff stopped at Rinaldi's. He was headed out to see if Willy Gleason had cleared off his mother's land. Since the volunteer fire department is about as close as he'll come to having a deputy, a few of us went along.

There had been a problem, though. When Vallina Gleason heard the sheriff had ordered Willy off her property, she put up such a fuss they thought they were going to have a first-class riot right there in the hospital. Word was, even after they'd given her a couple of hefty shots to quiet her down she was sitting up in bed moaning, "My boy. My Willy. They're taking my Willy from me." When a nurse reminded her that he had tried to kill her, she said, "He never hurt nobody. He likes to have a little fun, that's all." This was her thirty-year-old son she was talking about, the one with the shotgun and the snake eyes. The one who held burning cigarettes in his bare hand.

So now the sheriff was in something of a bind, since

the old lady swore she didn't want Willy kicked out.

"My mistake was sticking my nose in their business in the first place," the sheriff told us. "I should have left them alone to kill each other off, if that's what they wanted to do." But he was worried about his reputation. He couldn't go around giving orders, he said, then not following through on them. So we drove out there, and even then we could see how the Gleason business was beginning to wear him down.

The first thing that took us was finding Sylvia Biddle sitting alone with her legs dangling off the porch, nobody else in sight. Moved right in, I figured. When we got a little closer, we saw she was holding a baby, and that about did us in. "I'll be damned," Clarky kept saying. "I'll be god-damned."

But Aldin, who's always got an answer for everything, said, "How you know that ain't one of Vallina's babies?" We didn't know, since the old lady had started having them when she was thirteen or so, and there was no telling when she'd stop. We stared hard at that baby, trying to figure it out. It could have been Sylvia and Willy's, it could have been Vallina and the old man's, and if it was possible, it could have belonged to all four of them.

Sylvia acted like it was the most natural thing in the world to see us out there. She was chewing—bubble gum or something—swinging her legs, and holding that kid on her knee like it was a bag of dirty laundry and she was waiting for an empty machine at the laundromat.

"Where's Willy?" the sheriff asked.

She looked at him like she didn't understand, and when he asked again, she pointed real slow to the trees at the end of the lot and said, "In the *shed,*" like there was something wrong with us that we didn't naturally know where he was.

Never mind we couldn't see a shed, we headed where she'd pointed. I think we all tensed up a bit as we walked across that lawn, thinking any minute somebody was going to take a shot at us.

When we got down near the trees we heard hammering, and when we started into the woods we saw a rundown shack about twenty yards in. Sheriff called out, "Willy Gleason, you in there?" The hammering stopped and half a minute later Willy came out.

He stood with a cigarette hanging from his bottom lip, his eyes squinting. "What?" he said, and the cigarette didn't move.

"Like to know what you're up to," the sheriff said.

"Fixing," he answered.

"You've been doing a lot of that lately," the sheriff said. "I thought I told you to be off your mother's place."

"I'm off it," Willy Gleason said.

He was right about that. The Gleason property went as far as the trees. Sullivan owned the rest. Sullivan's kids must have built the shack to play in a good seven or eight years ago. Willy had hauled out an old mattress, one that had probably been inside that shack all those years, through the snow and rain and rats and woodchucks. We had a pretty good idea that he was fixing up his honeymoon cottage.

"Sullivan know you're on his land?" the sheriff asked.

Willy shrugged. "Beats me," he said. Clarky started to laugh, but the sheriff gave him a look.

The sheriff eyed that shack like he was stumped. Then he said to Willy, "I believe you *could* live in there."

Willy said nothing, just looked down at the dirt like we weren't there.

Then the sheriff hitched up his pants. "I'll tell you one thing, Gleason. Your mother's coming back home, which you may not be too happy about, but I don't give a damn about that. I don't want to hear another word from you clowns out here. I don't want to be called out here again for nothing. Next time I'll lock you up a lot longer than overnight."

If Willy was supposed to answer, nobody had told him about it. He stood with his head down, probably thinking how he was going to have to find a sheet of plastic to put over the roof for when it rained.

So we left, and by the time we reached our cars, the sheriff was swearing up a storm about how he had better things to do with his time than referee a herd of idiots. The rest of us got in Clarky's car, and we weren't but half a mile down the road when all four of us broke loose laughing, even stone-faced Aldin.

The way Willy stood there and swore he was off his mother's property reminded us of the way he had blasted away at his mother as if it was the right and natural thing to do. And that got us reminiscing about a few other Glea-son gems. By the time we reached Rinaldi's, we were well into the greased pig fiasco, but that's another story.

From what Early told us, it looked like Willy was done fixing up his honeymoon cottage and Sylvia had moved in. Pete said you could make out where a path was starting to wear across the lawn, between the porch to those woods. He'd spot Willy out there, near those trees, smoking his cigarettes.

The old lady was sent home from the hospital but, even so, things stayed quiet for a while. We didn't see any of the Gleasons in town much, except once in a while, down at Coleman's buying cigarettes or candy or soft drinks. The old man, of course, was in and out as usual for his beer.

It was a Tuesday morning when we got the news about him. I can't say that anyone was much surprised. Shorty Bova's kid was headed for his new job at the milk plant, about five-thirty A.M., walking, because that last DWI he got had cost him his license. Halfway down Canal Street, almost to Osgood's, he saw something in the canal that didn't belong there. When he got closer he could see it was a man. Once he got his legs back, he turn-tailed it for the municipal building, which of course was closed, looking for the sheriff. By the time he flagged down May Hammer, just beginning the day's rounds in her one-woman taxi operation, he was barely able to talk sense. May radioed for the sheriff and state police, and by six A.M. we had a full-blown carnival down on Canal Street. The sheriff, troopers, ambulance, Diefendorf from the *Journal*, clicking away with his camera, two fire trucks, and half the town came out to watch Old Man Gleason get fished out of the canal.

He was dead, of course. Had been for some time. We figured he must have bought a six-pack at last call and sat on the canal bank to finish it off. The carton lay on its side with the empties scattered around. One bottle, unopened, sat in the tipped-over carton.

I've seen dead men before, plenty of them. And I've seen two drowned men. But Gleason is the only one I can honestly say looked just the same drowned and dead as he looked alive.

Naturally, the county paid for the funeral. The Gleason clan trooped into town, single file, scrubbed and dressed in what must have been their good clothes. The old lady sweated and huffed along in the lead. Sylvia Biddle followed at the end of the line, carrying that round-headed baby. And Willy shuffled about twenty feet behind the rest, kicking up dust. They looked mournful and lost, marching like that, a string of ducks.

They gathered outside the Presbyterian church, even though no one had ever seen a Gleason step inside the place before. The old lady seemed drugged as she clutched one of her kids' hands in each of hers. She let out a moan. "Daddy's gone," she said, talking to no one, just making a statement to the air. "Daddy's gone," she said again, real quiet. Her kids tugged at her, and she followed them into the church. Willy stayed outside, pacing up and down the sidewalk, smoking. Every once in a while he'd sneak a glance at the hearse parked at the curb, like it was something alive and he was checking to see if it had moved.

Grief it was, and it surprised me. They have feelings for each other, too, I realized, just like anyone else.

After the service they moved outside for the trip to the cemetery. The pallbearers were having a time getting the casket into the hearse, partly because the old man was heavy, partly because nobody knew what they were doing. While they struggled with the back doors that kept swinging shut on them, the kids raised hell, running and chasing each other, wild from sitting still in church. So nobody noticed when the one they call Francis climbed in the driver's seat. When he started the engine, I suppose everyone just figured it was the driver, since they'd just managed to get the casket in, although they hadn't yet figured out how to get the doors shut. The hearse lurched away, with the doors swinging behind.

The kid couldn't drive, naturally. Things might have been different if he could see, but as it was, his head didn't quite reach the top of the dash. It's a miracle no one was run over. Half a dozen men took off down the street on foot, shouting after the hearse.

The ride was short. The kid swung wide onto Canal Street, and down they went, the Gleason boy, the dead man, and Lou Grasso's brand-new fifteen-thousand-dollar hearse, into the canal. The boy made it out the window and waded to the bank, looking scared, but grinning too, mud and weeds dripping from him. The hearse lay nose down, with just its rear fender showing. And for the second time in three days the fire department was called to fish Old Man Gleason out of the canal.

And that was that. After we got the hearse pulled out, and finally got the old man buried, the Gleasons went back to their house on the mucklands, and we didn't hear anything more for a good several months. That's not counting the week the Catholic sisters took up a food and clothing collection and the three of them made a field trip out there. But that's another story altogether.

Once the Gleasons did venture back into town for groceries, they were quiet about it. So it was a while before we began to notice the change taking place in Willy. He let his hair grow, and he started growing a beard and mustache, too. Then he got rid of his shoes. It was November and he was still walking the roads barefoot. During the winter we didn't see any of them much, but a couple people swore Willy was at the laundromat in February, barefoot, and with a head of hair like a grizzly.

Then, just like that, we had one of those rare spring days when the temperature hit seventy and it seemed like summer, with everyone out, walking, raking their lawns, and visiting. Willy and Sylvia came to town, pushing their baby in a stroller. Willy's scraggly beard reached halfway down his chest, and his hair fell over his shoulders. He was barefoot, and he wore a heavy winter jacket, zipped up to the neck. Everyone else was in shirt sleeves, Sylvia and the baby too, it was that warm.

When they came out of Coleman's store, Sylvia un-wrapped two orange Popsicles and gave one to the kid, while Willy tucked a new pack of Lucky Strikes into his jacket pocket. They sat on the summer bench Coleman had just hauled outside the store. The kid teetered around on bowlegs, drooling over its Popsicle, while Sylvia sucked on her own with a dumb, dreamy look. Willy smoked.

Then, of course, the kid dropped the Popsicle in the dirt and started screaming over it. Sylvia tried to clean the thing off, then she offered part of her own, but the kid wouldn't let up. Willy lifted the kid, and he held it so it stood on his lap facing him. He stared at it. That's all. The baby went rigid, and dead silent, not even a sniffle, while it stared right back into Willy's crazy eyes. I saw it happen. So did Grove and a few others.

After that, people started saying Willy almost looked like Jesus, what with the hair and the bare feet. But some were outraged over the comparison and insisted that if he looked like anything it was a lunatic, and a dangerous one at that.

A month or so later we sat at Rinaldi's, talking. Both Aldin and Clarky were killing time, waiting for their social security checks, which were a day late. Grove was up front helping Rinaldi fill tin buckets with nails.

Clarky looked at the clock, then he called out to Grove, "Early go by yet?"

"Nope," he said. Then he said, "Why you so worried about money, Clarky? Don't you trust your government?"

"I got to eat, don't I?" Clarky said. "I got to pay my bills."

It was about that time the fire whistle sounded, two-two, out of town. We jumped into Grove's truck, all four of us wedging into the front seat, and we left Rinaldi setting out his buckets of brads and roofing nails.

We swung down Center Street and headed for the station, to follow the trucks out. Eddie Townsend was just getting behind the wheel of the pumper when we eased alongside. He waved us ahead and shouted, "Sawbuck Road. The Gleason house." We took off.

"Jesus Almighty," Clarky said. "Now what?"

We were halfway there when Grove let out a low whistle. He pointed north, beyond Hixson's alfalfa lot and the trees edging the Squashalone, and we saw it, a chimney cloud of black smoke. Grove stepped on it, and we didn't say another word until the pickup jumped the ditch and rocked to a halt on the Gleason lawn.

All that showed through the fire were the two-by-fours that used to hold the inside walls, and the stairway leading to the second story. Even from inside the truck we felt the heat. We got out, and the air was loud with the sound of burning. Above the flames the black smoke, thick with cinders and bits of wood, rolled up into the sky. We had to shout to be heard over the roaring flames and splintering wood. Pretty soon it started snowing cinders.

We hauled a couple hoses out and turned the water on, knowing full well it was no use. Finally the chief shouted over for us to wet the trees and lawn and let the fire burn itself out.

The Gleasons and Sylvia Biddle stood off to the side, watching. The kids didn't say anything except when the stairway collapsed. One of the boys pointed to it and said,

"There she goes." It fell apart in midair, just disappeared into the flames.

But the old lady wailed and paced and called for her dead husband. Just before the stairs went, she tried to run back into the burning house, calling out for the old man to hurry and get out. We tackled her and dragged her back. The sheriff kept an eye on her. He kept telling her, "Chester's all right. He's not in the house. He's down at Osgood's, remember?"

"Chester's all right?" she asked him.

"He's not in the house," the sheriff kept telling her. "He's in town, at Osgood's."

The fire soon eased up. There was nothing left to burn. That's when we noticed the chicken coop or, I should say, what used to be the chicken coop. A few wisps of smoke rose from a black square burned onto the ground. We counted five chicken skeletons, the bones charred black. Then we saw that the woods beyond were on fire, too.

We moved the truck out there, fast, and started pumping. Once we got things under control, we could see it was the honeymoon shack that had started the trees off. And since the shack was so far from the house, we knew right then the fires had been set. A couple of cinder blocks, one hunk of mattress, and a rusted barrel with a length of stovepipe jammed into a hole cut in its side were all that remained.

Of course, the sheriff asked plenty of questions, but he didn't get any answers. The old lady was too far gone to make sense. Her kids were too busy jumping over the fire hoses and slinging mud at each other from the puddles to bother talking to anyone about why their house had just burned to the ground. Sylvia stood in a trance, holding her sleeping kid. When the kid started drooling down the sleeve of her blouse she moved it to the other hip.

Willy smoked his cigarettes. He had watched the whole thing with a calm, interested expression. The sheriff tried to question him, but all he did was shrug his shoulders and say, "I don't know nothing." He kept his eyes on the smoldering house when he spoke.

It was Clarky who found the gasoline cans. He brought them over, two of them, and set them down between Willy and the sheriff, without saying a word. Willy glanced at them, then back at the house.

The sheriff shook his head. "It's just about what I expected," he said in a tired voice. "You done it now, Gleason. This one's for keeps."

Willy stood as if he hadn't heard anything. Then, without turning his head, he flicked his burning cigarette toward one of the gasoline cans, and it was about six inches from dropping into the opening when Clarky jumped and sent the can flying with a kick of his boot, the fastest I've ever seen him move.

The sheriff jumped too. "Crazy bastard," he yelled, and he punched Willy in the jaw. Willy's head swung to one side with the force of the blow while the rest of his body stayed stock-still. Then he turned his head back until his eyes met the sheriff's. Willy looked worn out, but most of all he looked—dignified. That's the only word for it, wild hair and crazy eyes notwithstanding. He let himself be handcuffed, and the sheriff had two of us ride with him as he took Willy over to the county jail.

The fire made our town famous. At least for a week or so it did. Once the word "arson" got out, we had people in here from the city newspaper and TV stations, doing interviews, taking pictures, asking questions. There were other people, too, the ones who drove in on a Saturday or Sunday to have a look at the burned-down Gleason place, and hear the stories that by that time were circulating around. One story told of a religious fanatic who had direct orders from God to burn his house down with all his family inside as punishment for the Gleason no one had known about, the one that had been kept locked in a broom closet for twenty years. Another version told of Willy burning just himself up in the house, as a sacrifice for the town's sins. That version included finding thousands of dollars stuffed into canning jars buried in the cellar.

Then, as fast as it started, it stopped. The welfare trucked the Gleasons down to Hiram, in the southern tip of the county, to live in a renovated house near the state's adult shelter. But Sylvia Biddle stayed. She moved back into the Beehive apartments in town, taking the fat-headed kid with her. So it was just Vallina Gleason and her brood down there in Hiram. All of them except Willy.

Willy stayed in the county jail a few days, until they sent him off somewhere for mental tests. Word was they'd locked him up in a prison for the criminally insane.

So they were gone, those Gleasons. They weren't missed at Sunday church services, and their kids weren't missed on the playground or little league field and, needless to say, none of the stores felt a dip in proceeds because of them. But something had changed, just the same. I'd call it a loss, of some sort. Maybe a loss of heritage would be the right way to put it. Good or bad, those Gleasons belonged to this town.

Now, whenever we drove out there on Sawbuck Road and got a look at that charred place where the house used to be, and the black hole of the cellar half-filled with rotting wood and broken chimney bricks, we'd get to thinking about the Gleasons and what they were up to in that new house of theirs in Hiram.

Grove heard that the old lady dropped dead of a heart attack shortly after the move, supposedly because she couldn't take living in a strange town so far from where her husband was buried. But nobody could say for sure if it was true. And Aldin had it from a cousin in Albany that Willy Gleason had already escaped from the prison for the criminally insane.

We were at Rinaldi's, talking about it, in between Clarky going on about his social security and Grove telling how the doctor said it was arthritis of the spine, not lumbago, that he had.

"No wheelchair for me," Grove said. "Shoot me first. I mean it."

"Sure," Aldin told him. "I know somebody'd love to do it, too, just for the fun of it."

"I wonder what he's up to," Clarky said. He shook his head, thinking. "I hope to Christ he doesn't come back here starting trouble."

"There's nothing in this town he wants," Grove said. "It's his mama he's after, not you. Not her, either."

He pointed out the window to where Sylvia Biddle was trying to get a baby stroller, with that fat-headed kid of hers in it, over the curb. Never mind the kid was big enough to walk. The stroller was a clumsy old-fashioned model, with one wheel about ready to come off. Sylvia leaned into the stroller, her rear end sticking out in one direction, and her scrawny arms in the other direction. She rocked that buggy, trying to swing it around, pushing like her life depended on it, trying to get over that damn curb.

"You think the old lady's really dead?" Rinaldi said.

"Don't know," Aldin said.

"Hard to believe," said Clarky.

"We should all take a ride down there to Hiram," I told them. "Just to see."

"I was thinking that myself," Grove said.

Clarky snapped shut his pocket watch that he'd been checking against Rinaldi's wall clock. He put the watch back in his pocket. "Remember the Gleason girl," he said, "how she looked, greased head to toe, when she caught the pig?"

"How about the time the old man fell asleep drunk in Tucker's onion warehouse and then couldn't get out?"

Aldin sat back through it all as we talked, tamping on his pipe, nodding his head a little. You might almost call it a smile he had on that face of his.

"Look there," Aldin said, motioning with the pipe out the window. "You ever think of that?"

Sylvia managed the stroller over the curb. She kicked at the bad wheel to knock it back in place.

"What?" Grove said.

"The kid," Aldin said. "We still got Willy Gleason's kid." He looked pleased, all right, that Aldin.

And we sat there thinking about it as we watched Sylvia and the kid move down the sidewalk. Then they turned and disappeared into Coleman's store.

HUNTERS

She was glad it was getting dark because now the shooting would stop. It had made them jumpy for a couple of days, sounding so close. She was afraid to go out of the house. She'd even made George call the sheriff when it had started. But the sheriff said unless their property was posted there wasn't anything he could do. It was always like this in hunting season. And now, today, it was worse than ever.

"I'm afraid they're going to shoot toward the house and hit one of us," Alice told her husband.

"Maybe I should post the land, like the sheriff said," he answered.

"You've been saying that."

"I'm going to town first thing in the morning," George told her. "I'm getting some signs, and I'm putting them up, but good. Then we'll see."

"I didn't know it was going to be like this," Alice said. "If I'd known—"

He looked at her with that worried look he got whenever she was at the end of her patience with him.

It had been one thing after another since they'd moved in. First she'd found out she was pregnant. Then he'd lost his job. And everything was strange between them lately.

"Maybe we should go stay with my mother," she said.

"This is our house," George told her. "This is where we should stay."

She stood near the window, resting her hands on her round stomach. "We should never have moved here," she said.

"You liked it," he told her. "You said you wanted to live here."

"I didn't think it would be so—deserted. I didn't know we'd be living in the middle of a wilderness."

"Well, don't blame me now. You said you liked it."

She turned and looked him straight in the eye. "I *do* blame you. I feel like I'm in prison. In solitary confinement."

He raised his eyebrows. "With me?" he said, and he smiled.

"It was bad enough when you worked," she told him. "But now, when you're gone all day with your friends. And at night, too."

"Just once in a while," he said. "Not all the time. Don't I ask you to come?"

"I hate those places. I hate bars. You said you wouldn't anymore."

"I have to have some fun, don't I? What am I supposed to do, just sit around here day and night?"

"Like I do?" she said. "You could get a job."

"There *aren't* any jobs."

She turned from him. "Something's not right," she said.

He came up behind her and put his hand on her stomach. "The baby?" he asked, sounding a little startled.

"I don't mean that."

She looked out the window. "They've stopped," she told him.

"It must be too dark for them now."

"Good," she said.

She turned and faced him. "I want to stay with my mother, George. Just for a while. Till the baby comes."

"God, Alice," he said. "She'd just love that, wouldn't she?"

"I've talked to her," she told him.

"And what about me? Am I invited, too?"

She didn't answer.

He ran his hand through his hair. He moved away from her and sat down at the kitchen table, his head in his hands. "Sit down with me," he told her. "Come sit with me for a minute."

She went and stood near the table, facing him.

"Gil needs a driver," he told her. "It's not full-time, but it's something."

"Did you tell him yes?"

"I'll tell him tomorrow."

"I can't take much more of this, George."

"I'm telling him, Alice. I'm telling him tomorrow."
She sat down with him.

"You have to be twenty-one, though," he said. "I told him I'm twenty-one."

She gazed across the room, and she touched her stomach, and moved her fingers across it.

"Is he kicking?" George asked.

"Yes."

"I'm going to cook you the best supper you ever had," he told her. "You never had anything like this, I swear." He got up from the table and went to the refrigerator.

"What are you talking about? You don't know how to cook." She didn't know if she would laugh or get angry.

"But I do, I do," he answered. He waltzed around the kitchen, cradling a chicken wrapped in cellophane.

"George," she said, and she laughed, in spite of herself. Her laughter spurred him on, and he danced with the chicken for her. Then he waltzed back to her and put the chicken on the table. "We need mushrooms."

She got up and went to the cupboard and took out a can of mushrooms. She helped him cook. They turned the radio on while they ate supper, and they didn't talk anymore about her moving in with her mother.

It was still early. He sat on the floor, polishing his boots over a newspaper. She had set the ironing board up in the living room and was ironing a shirt for him.

"It's only Gil," he told her.

"And what if he's already got somebody? And you have to go look somewhere else?"

He gave her a funny look and shook his head, and she knew that work was the furthest thing from his mind.

She put the shirt on a hanger and hooked it over a doorknob. She stopped and watched him bent over the boots, steadily rubbing the polish in. The oddest thing had been happening to her lately: The bigger the baby grew inside her, the emptier she felt.

She heard the sound again, and looked toward the door. "George, what *is* that? Do you hear it?"

"What?" He kept his head lowered.

"It sounds like somebody walking outside."

He looked up and listened, and she watched his face. He went back to polishing the boots. "Probably deer the hunters scared up."

She moved quietly through the room, straining to listen for sounds, as she put away her ironing things. Even the house felt empty—cool and damp and echoing, out in the middle of the empty woods.

When he'd finished with the boots, they both heard the sound. "That's not deer," she told him.

"Somebody's out there," he said.

"Who can it be? Tom?" she said, thinking of their neighbor a half mile down the road. "I didn't hear any car."

He shook his head. They listened as the footsteps came nearer.

"Who is it?" George called out.

There was no answer.

"Who's out there?" he called again. "Tom?"

"We need help," a voice said.

George stood up. Alice folded her hands against her stomach and watched the door.

"What is it?" George asked. "What kind of help?" He took a step closer to the door.

"Open up," the man said. "We got lost in the woods. Hunting."

"Lost?" Alice said to George.

"Hey!" the man called. "Can we use your phone?"

"George," Alice said.

He looked at her. "It's all right," he told her. "Isn't it?" He called to the man, "You want to use the phone?"

"Yeah," the man said.

George looked at Alice again and shrugged. He went and opened the door.

She was able to see the man from where she stood. He was heavy, with a stubbly beard, and he carried a shotgun. His jacket was half-zipped, with a plaid flannel shirt showing underneath.

"Got dark on us," the man said. He peered around George, into the room.

"Petey," a voice close behind him said.

"It's okay," the man said.

They entered the house. The other man was smaller. He cradled his left arm, wrapped in a thick wad of cloth. He was bald, and his face was strange, pale and wrinkled like a baby's. Yet he looked like he couldn't have been over thirty. He walked in behind Petey, moving his eyes quickly to take in everything.

George closed the door.

Petey looked around the room. When he noticed Alice, he nodded to her. She couldn't keep her eyes off the other one's hand. "Had a little accident," Petey told them.

"The phone's over there," George said.

"Mind if we sit down a minute?" Petey asked. "We've been on our feet all day."

He sat on the sofa. The other man stood quietly, swaying a little, holding his left hand. Petey leaned back on the sofa, the shotgun propped between his knees.

"Coe," the man said. "Have a seat." Coe didn't move.

"You all right?" Petey asked him.

"Yeah."

"You better sit down," Petey told him.

"I'm okay," Coe said, but he sat in the chair across from Petey anyway.

"Wasn't expecting to find a couple of kids living out here," Petey said. "Thought the place was still empty."

"Do you want me to call somebody for you?" George asked the man.

"No, that's all right," Petey told him.

"George," Alice said from the far side of the room.

"George," the man repeated. His eyes were half-closed, as if he were exhausted. "Now there's a name you don't hear too often. Used to be popular, though." He moved his knees so that the gun fell against his stomach. "Ain't that right, Coe?"

"Yeah, that's right," Coe said. "You got any food here?"

Alice looked at George, expecting him to do something. But George acted like nothing was wrong.

"We've been out here all day," Petey said to him. "We haven't eaten since early morning."

"It's okay, Alice," George said to her. "Can't you find them something?"

"Thank you, George," Petey said.

Alice kept her eyes on George a minute, to let him know what she thought of him.

When she started for the kitchen, Petey leaned forward and watched her. "Well," he said to George. "Looks like you kids have been keeping yourselves busy out here."

Alice hurried from the room.

"She's pumped right up there, isn't she?" the man said.

She was horrified.

"You said you wanted to use the phone," George told the man. She could hear them through the open doorway. "There's the phone."

She cut pieces of cold chicken and threw the sandwiches together. There was no outside door in the kitchen, but there was a window. She looked up at it, considering, but they would be able to see her through the doorway.

"You said you were lost," she heard George say. His voice shook a little. "You said you needed help."

"That's right," Petey answered. "That's what I said. How's that hand, Coe?"

"It's all right."

Alice found a tray and put the sandwiches on it. She paused in the doorway with it.

"George, I wonder if you could bring us all a little something to drink," Petey said. "You're old enough to drink, aren't you? A little bourbon would be nice."

George looked up at Alice. "You better go now," he told the man, "if you're not going to use the phone."

"You're funny," Petey told him.

Alice set the tray down on the end table. Already pieces of chicken were falling from between the slices of bread. "Do you know that, ma'am?" Petey said. "Do you know how funny your boyfriend is?"

Alice stepped away from him. She looked the man in the eye. She wanted him out of her house now.

"It's good to have a sense of humor," Petey told her. "Coe," he said, "you better eat something." He laid the shotgun at his feet and picked up a sandwich.

"Alice," Petey said. "Could you take this tray to Coe? I don't think he can get up."

Alice took the tray to Coe and held it angrily in front of him. Coe glanced at her as he picked up a sandwich, and she backed away from him. He ate with his one good hand.

Alice watched the wrinkles move over his strange face as he chewed.

"Now where's that drink?" Petey said. "George, didn't you just bring me a drink?"

George hesitated. He went to the cupboard near the kitchen doorway and brought out a bottle and two glasses. "You've got to leave after this," he told the men. He put the bottle and glasses down next to the tray.

"That's right," Petey said. He filled the glasses, and the two of them drank and ate in silence.

The door across the room seemed a long way off. Alice looked at George while the men ate. And then, like that, George and Alice began to move, slowly, carefully, toward the door. George reached out and lightly touched her arm, but she was not afraid. The men had no right to be there, and she wanted them out.

George and Alice were at the other end of the sofa, and still the men paid them no attention. Then they were near the door, without having made a sound, and they moved toward the door, almost there.

The gun exploded, and Alice cried out from the noise of it. A piece of wall shattered to bits of flying wood and plaster in front of them.

They froze, then turned around.

"It's not polite to walk out on your company," Petey said.

A puff of smoke hung near Petey. Alice could smell the burned powder and splintered wood. Coe looked at her over the rim of his glass.

"Come sit here with me," Petey told them. His voice sounded so odd after the blast. He motioned with the gun.

George finally moved and sat where the man had pointed.

"You, too, honey," Petey said.

She kept her eyes on George, but he did not look at her. She moved awkwardly across the room; it seemed to take her forever. They are going to shoot us now, she thought, and she felt sad, not for herself or for George, but for the baby.

Petey filled Coe's glass for him, then sat back down. Coe drank and let out a sigh.

"You hurting, Coe?" Petey asked.

"No."

"Honey, why don't you go get us some bandages? And something to clean out that wound, some antiseptic."

"I'm okay," Coe said.

It took Alice a minute to realize they weren't going to be killed right then. She looked at George. He sat clasping his knees, gazing down at the floor as if he were afraid to make the slightest move, leaving it all up to her. It had always been that way, she knew it, but it struck her now how nothing she could do would ever change him. And that was what her mother had been trying to tell her about him all along.

"You ever been hunting?" Petey asked George.

"No," George blurted.

She started for the bathroom, in a daze, still feeling the shock of the shotgun blast. She took gauze and antiseptic from the cabinet, and a towel that she wet, and came back into the room.

"Everybody should know how to shoot a gun," Petey said. "Right, Coe?"

Alice stood with the bandages in front of Coe. His head was thrown back, and his eyes were closed.

"Coe," Petey said. "Let Alice fix your hand. Coe!"

He stirred.

"She's going to fix that hand, Coe," Petey told him. "Go ahead," he said to her.

George rose to help. "Let me do that," he said. "Leave her out of this."

"George, I think you should calm down. Alice is doing a fine job. You're doing a fine job, Alice." Petey lifted the shotgun and examined the barrel. He squinted at George over the barrel. "Sit down," he told him.

"Now, Alice," Petey said, "take that rag off Coe's hand. Clean his hand up nice, and put a new bandage on for him." He nodded to encourage her.

Alice knelt on the floor and began to unwrap Coe's hand. He sat with his head tilted back, eyeing her. She could not bear touching him. She tried to hurry, to get it over with. When the rag was almost off, he winced. The blood was everywhere.

"Jesus," George said.

Alice wiped away blood with the wet towel. "It won't stop bleeding," she said.

"Just wrap it up," Petey told her.

Coe breathed hard while she dabbed at the wound.

"This is awful," Alice said. "This is bad."

"Them damn hunters," Petey said. "Must've thought Coe was a deer." He laughed. "We'll have to report this to the sheriff." He laughed again. "Won't we, Coe?"

They fell silent. Alice wrapped the hand in a clean bandage. Coe lay back in the chair with his eyes closed as she finished.

"Looks like you're due just about anytime," Petey said to her.

She glanced at him, then went back to the hand.

She could feel his eyes on her.

"A funny thing happened to me once when I was hunting," Petey said, after a while.

Alice left everything on the floor and went to George. He took her hand, and his palms were cold and damp.

"I killed a deer," Petey said. He turned and poured himself another drink. "This was a couple years ago.

"I went to gut it, right there in the woods. When I slit its belly open, you know what I found inside?"

He leaned forward and peered around George at Alice. Then he sat back again.

"That's right," he said. "Still alive, too."

George stood. "I want you to get the hell out of here."

"Now, George," Petey said. "I can't go anywhere with Coe like that."

They looked at Coe. He lay sprawled in the chair, with his eyes closed. His face was flushed, and he breathed heavily.

"Wake him up," George said.

"I couldn't do that," Petey answered. "He's had a rough day."

"Get the hell out of my house," George said.

Petey stood and walked over to the blood-soaked rags. He held the shotgun loosely in one arm as he looked down at the rags and nudged them with his foot. Then he turned to George and Alice and shook his head. "It's a shame what happens when you get careless," he told them.

Petey motioned with the gun. "George," he said, "I'd like you to move over this way a bit and have a seat, right there on the sofa. Move," he said. "Now."

He waited until George moved. "That's better," Petey said.

"For God's sakes, what do you want with us?" Alice cried.

Petey looked at her a moment, then moved toward her. When he was inches away, he reached his hand out to touch her. She gave a cry and jumped back.

Petey swung the shotgun around, before George had a chance to move.

"Leave her alone," George pleaded. "If you have to mess with somebody, mess with me."

His voice was weak. His face, too, was childish, and she was ashamed for him.

"George," Petey said, shaking his head. He shifted the angle of the shotgun. "I'm disappointed in you." He looked at her. "I'll bet Alice is, too."

She felt something rising up inside her, ready to spill over. She would not cry, she told herself.

"Look, you've upset poor Alice," Petey said to him.

"Go away," Alice pleaded. "Just go away."

Petey sat on the arm of the sofa. "I didn't think you were a crier," he said. He watched her for a while.

"That's an awfully pretty dress you're wearing," he said. "Why don't you move over there where I can see it better?" He motioned to the center of the room.

"Leave us alone," she said.

"Right over there, Alice. You're not going to be difficult, are you?"

"Do it," George told her, in that terrified voice.

She moved to the center of the room and stood looking at George.

Petey turned so that he faced them. "I've got a wife," he told them. He nodded. "That's right." He moved his hand and rested it on the shotgun. "I always felt bad, though, that I was never able to buy her nice things." He nodded his head, thinking. "Like that pretty dress. Now that's what I'd call nice."

She turned her face away.

"What she wouldn't give to have a dress like that," Petey said.

"Please," George said to him.

"I just thought of something," Petey said. "Alice, wouldn't it be good of you to give me that dress for my wife? Because she never had nice things like you?"

"I'll give you money," George said. "The car."

"Alice, would you take that pretty dress off, please?" Petey said.

She was angry that she could not stop crying. She should have tried to get out the kitchen window when she was making sandwiches. She should have left before.

"Now, Alice," Petey said. "Take the dress off now."

George started from his seat.

Petey lifted the shotgun. "We don't want anyone getting hurt, George," he said. "Alice, do you want me to help you?"

She raised her hands to the buttons and looked at George. He shook his head at her, then turned his face away.

Something in her broke. She stopped the crying. She began unbuttoning the dress while she looked at George with a cold, hard look.

She could feel Petey watch her as she stepped out of the dress. She stood in her bra and half-slip holding the dress, not taking her eyes from George. He would not look at her. He was the one who had let them in. And now there was nothing either of them could do. The elastic stretched around her stomach, and she felt herself huge and exposed and grotesque.

"Come here, Alice," Petey said to her in a low voice. "Give me the dress."

She moved stiffly and handed it to him. His face was grave. "Still warm," he said.

When he looked at her, she saw how deep his sickness went. "Right here," he said. He pointed, high near her breastbone, then ran his thumb straight down over the curve of her stomach. "Like that," Petey said.

"God, please," George cried.

Alice stepped away from him. She was stone.

"George," Petey said, keeping his eyes on Alice, "do you like her like this? You know what I mean."

George didn't answer.

"What's it like?" Petey asked him. "How do you do it when she's like this?"

"Oh God," George cried.

Alice stood motionless. Everything was gone from her.

"Take your pants off," Petey told him.

A strangled sound came from the boy.

Petey lifted the shotgun and flicked the safety back and forth. "I said take them off."

Alice watched George take the pants off and drop them on the floor. He stood in his underwear, his legs thin and white.

"You want to kiss her first, don't you, George?" Petey told him.

For a minute she forgot herself: He was coming to her, and she would comfort him. But then he gave her a dead, cold kiss and pulled away.

"Get her down there on the floor," Petey said. "You can't do anything standing up."

George put his arms around her, awkwardly. She tried to look into his eyes, but he kept his head turned away. At last he got her on the floor. She felt the sides of her stomach fall in a little, and the baby move, then settle. It was such an odd thing to be lying there on the floor.

"Now get on top of her," she heard Petey tell George. But it didn't make any sense. They were in their underclothes.

"Watch out for that stomach," Petey said, and he laughed.

And then George whimpered.

George was a big shot, her mother said, always in the middle of whatever didn't concern him. When he came home late, Alice would have to listen to his stories of how so-and-so would have spent the night in a snowbank if he hadn't come along; or how someone else would have blown his garage to kingdom come if George hadn't noticed the gas leak. And all the while he was telling her his face got brighter and his voice louder while she would be thinking, I can't stand my life. I am going to die right now from the emptiness of it.

"You've got to move," Petey told George. "Show me how you move when you do it."

"God," George cried.

She heard Petey cross the room and sit on the arm of Coe's chair.

And George was above her, crying, while Petey kept the shotgun on him. George held himself up with his arms, trying not to touch her. He kept his face turned away from her.

But she loved him. That, too, made her angry. If it *was* love. She didn't know anything anymore. She touched his face, and he turned his eyes on her with such a look of horror that she drew back, stunned.

"George," she whispered, but he had already left.

"I don't think George really likes Alice," Petey said to the sleeping Coe. "What do you think, Coe?"

Petey crossed the room and stood over them a moment. He kicked violently at George.

"Get the hell off her," Petey shouted. "Don't you know anything?"

George crouched on the floor, away from Alice.

Petey stood over her. She held herself still, waiting for his next blow. He looked down at her, then over at George. Then he turned and went to the window.

"Where's your car keys?" he said.

George started to get up.

"I said give me the goddamn keys."

George went to the phone stand and fumbled through things, until he found the keys.

Alice watched from the floor. She could not move. She was afraid to make a sound.

Petey grabbed the keys from George. "Put your pants on," he told him. "You look like a jackass."

George went to help Alice up, as if he were a stranger helping with her groceries. He sat her on the end of the sofa. When he reached for the dress, Petey took it from him. "It's mine," he said. "Remember?"

George found her a sweater. They could not look at each other. She let him hand the sweater to her, and she put it on herself.

Petey went to the window again. He turned to them. "I've got a problem here," he said, his voice agitated. He sat on the sofa, facing Coe.

"What am I going to do with Coe?" Petey said. "And you, George? And Alice?" He looked at her. "You should be nicer to Alice."

"Don't hurt her," George pleaded.

"Hurt her?" Petey said. "I've been trying to help her. You've got to stop wasting your time on her, George."

Petey shook his head and looked around the room.

"She's a little like Coe." He laughed, then stopped. "Both more trouble than they're worth."

He leaned toward Alice. "Alice," Petey called. "Alice."

She sat with her hands in her lap, enduring him. Her eyes fell on George's boots, neat and polished, standing against the wall. Everything she'd ever wanted seemed so foolish.

"See?" Petey said to George.

He stood abruptly. "Do you have a gun, George?"

"No," George answered, startled.

"Living out here in the woods like this with no gun? How about money? You must have some money."

"I told you, I'll give you anything. Just don't hurt us."

"Get the money, George."

He emptied his pockets.

"This is pitiful," Petey said. "I'll need more than this."

George found Alice's purse and took her wallet out. She watched the paper bills flutter between them.

"That's all, George?" Petey asked.

"I'm out of work. I been out of work a long time."

Petey shook his head. He looked at Alice and shook his head again.

He walked over to Coe and looked down at him, then turned to George. "Do you think we can trust Alice for a few minutes, George?"

"Don't shoot us," George pleaded.

Petey went to the phone. He picked it up and yanked, so that the cord snapped. "Get Coe," he said.

George looked at the man, afraid. Petey motioned with the shotgun. "Pick him up, George. Get him out of here."

George moved toward the unconscious man. He touched Coe's sleeve and pulled back.

"Hurry up, goddamnit," Petey yelled.

Alice watched George struggle to get the man from the chair. "He won't wake up," George said.

"Go on," Petey told him. "Move."

George dragged Coe to the door. He looked over his shoulder at her. "I'll be right back, Alice," he said. His voice was shaking.

She rose, as if to follow him.

Petey opened the door.

"George," Alice said.

"I'm coming back," George said. Petey nudged George out and slammed the door shut after them.

She heard them trying to get Coe into the car. And then the shotgun went off. Petey called out, "You bastard," then laughed. The car door slammed shut and the engine started. Then the car pulled away.

She stood for a long time, stunned, listening to the quiet. When she was finally able to move she went to the sofa and sat down across from the empty chair. The bloody rags lay nearby, and she could not take her eyes from them.

She'd known before she married him what she was getting herself into and she'd gone and done it anyway. There was something terribly wrong with her, she saw that now. She lay her hand on her stomach and wondered what in God's name she'd been doing her whole life.

And then she heard him outside, and it startled her. She knew George was out there. But she didn't know what she felt: relief or disappointment.

He came in and shut the door. She felt him standing there, awkward and embarrassed.

"Are you all right?" he said at last, so quietly she could barely hear.

"I don't know," she answered, without looking up. She couldn't look at him.

She heard him move toward her, then stop.

She was alone. Even the baby was hers alone. She had tried so hard to make it seem otherwise.

"I thought he was going to kill me," George said. He put his hand to his face and felt it.

She stared hard at him, until he finally seemed to notice her again. "I'll go get help," he told her. "I'll get Tom."

She shook her head. "I can't stay here."

He went and sat down in the chair across from her. "God," he said, running his hand through his hair. "Jesus."

"I told you," she said. And she held her breath, waiting to see if there was anything left between them.

GLASS

When we put our oldest girl on the bus to Buffalo where she had a job waiting at the Western Union, it was like a big storm let loose inside me and stirred up a lot of hard things. She sat with her elbow propped on the window ledge, the back of her hand pressed to the window to keep her face from our view, refusing us even a look, even that much of a good-bye. It dawned on me that my sullen child was not running off to a bright future like other girls, but was going to meet some new kind of misery. The flood broke, all twenty years' worth, for what I had done to her, what I had done to all my kids by giving them this hell for a life, which they would spend the rest of their days overcoming.

All because I said Yes. Yes I'll marry you. Yes I'll live in that godforsaken farmhouse that was so run-down it would have been an act of mercy if someone had come along with a bulldozer and plowed the whole thing under. And Yes I will live with your crazy brother, Carl, and your sister, Ruby, the worst Yes of all. It was love that blinded me, coming on so late in life. As if me wanting a little love was such a crime, something to pay for the rest of my life.

I looked over at Len. He had his hands shoved in his pockets, already turning back to the car, his head bowed, not in sadness over our scowling daughter who refused to wave good-bye, but in thought, figuring how he was going to get those thirty acres plowed when he'd just agreed to haul a load of Santini's onions to the pickling factory down near the Pennsylvania line. I had no right to blame him, not even for leaving me and the babies alone with Carl, since it was his lot in life to work, with six mouths to feed and one thing after another breaking down as soon as he thought he'd got a chance to take a breath.

And I could not blame Carl, since he did not choose to be that way, a grown man who talked to himself and talked to the dead and needed somebody to see that he washed, to see that he shaved and got dressed right.

And I could not blame myself anymore, since I'd been doing that all along, for not having the sense to see what living there would turn into.

I stood on the brink of that storm, not knowing which way it would take me—back to silent suffering or ahead to something new—afraid either way.

As the bus lumbered into traffic, leaving behind a cloud of exhaust, I lurched forward with it: I turned every-

thing on Ruby, once and for all, even though I had be-
grudged her from the start and said plenty of things about
her, right to Len's face, too. First, for not having the de-
cency to get out of our house. Then for going off to teach
and leaving me with Carl. Then for making more money
than she knew what to do with, money she couldn't bear
to part with, when she could see as well as anyone that we
could use a few groceries or the kids had holes in their
boots. And she was supposed to be so smart, the algebra
teacher.

Len walked ahead, humming to himself, unaware that
anything had happened to me. I dragged myself up behind
him out of that flooded river and made my decision to save
what was left of my life, and maybe the lives of the other
three kids as well: I decided that after all those years of
putting up with Ruby Mondo and her crazy brother Carl,
I would never again set foot in their house.

Which would be hard to do, considering we lived not
fifty yards from each other. Because when she saw that the
kids were getting to be too many and too big, she finally
moved out. She parted with some of that hoard of hers and
built a little house on a piece of Len's corn lot, smack across
the road, so that every time I opened the door I was reminded that I could not get away from her, from them,
reminded that even though we lived in that broken-down
farmhouse we called ours, it would never belong to us, no
matter what the mortgage papers said. Len never said a
word, and I never said a word. In that respect we were a
perfect match. We just let things happen.

As we drove home, I sat quiet. I watched the car
dealerships and the factories, and then the open fields slip
by, and little by little the peace eased into me. Even with
my one girl lost, I had hope for myself and the other three
kids at home. Len drummed his fingers on the steering

wheel, anxious to get back to the only life that made any sense to him: work.

And so I kept my resolve, which nobody knew about except me.

Still, she called on the phone as usual, wanting me to come over for one foolish thing or another. My excuses didn't faze her. She'd haul whatever it was over here, the mail she kept getting from motor vehicles that she never answered and couldn't figure out, that ended up telling her she'd been driving half a year with an expired license; or the thermos I had to look at to see why everything kept leaking out, when she'd broken the liner and had never thought to replace it. Things like that.

And as usual, too, they wandered in without knocking, whenever they pleased. Carl looking for his dog that had been dead a quarter of a century, yelling at me to get out of his house; Ruby pacing the kitchen, touching things, shredding up one of the kids' homework papers that'd been left on the table while she talked nonstop with no one but herself listening, all while I tried to mop the floor around them or do another load of wash or get supper on the table.

At least *I* knew I was staying away, even if nobody else did. And I felt good for it.

But maybe I wasn't cut out for feeling good.

I was nearly two months into my new life when she called with something in her voice that put me on guard. Her words weren't any different, but behind them I heard a storm brewing, heading my way, calling me by name to come out and see.

Whatever was up, I didn't want any part of it. "I'm in the middle of fixing supper," I lied.

"What, already? It'll only take a minute."

I told her I had fritters cooking and couldn't leave them. Then I worried that she'd come over and find nothing at all on the stove.

"I wouldn't have called if it wasn't important," she said. "You know that."

That was her lie.

But I began to wonder if something really was wrong, so wrong she couldn't speak it. "Is Carl all right?" I asked. For years we'd been waiting for him to drop dead, him being the way he was.

"Why certainly he's all right," she answered. "Why wouldn't he be?"

Then it dawned on me: I'd seen him, but she hadn't been over in a couple days. "Are you sick?"

"Sick?" She laughed. Then she didn't say anything, and that's when she had me. Because with Ruby Mondo there was never one moment of silence.

I fought anyway, knowing all the while it was a useless battle and I'd already lost. Time stretched out. I prayed that she'd hang up and find somebody else to bother.

But I heard her breathing on the other end, waiting for my answer.

I knew if I went and it was nothing, I'd be sorry. But if I didn't go over and it turned out to be something serious, I'd never forgive myself. Either way she had me.

I'm a terrible gambler. I've never won a thing in my life, not even an argument with myself. "I can only come over for a minute," I heard myself saying.

So it was done.

She let out a big sigh. "That's all it'll take," she said. Then, "Leonard's got a hammer, doesn't he? Bring the hammer."

Sometimes animals got into the chicken coop, looking

for eggs. Once, they sucked the insides out and left the shells; I'd never seen anything like it. That's what I was feeling like when I hung up the phone—those empty shells. Wanting me to come pound a nail for her when all she had to do was cross the road and get the hammer herself. Or wanting to use it as a weight for one of those idiotic school projects she was always gluing together, that her students rolled their eyes over.

As I scrounged for the hammer, cursing her and myself, I began to think maybe she was smarter than I'd given her credit for. Maybe she knew I was staying away and had been working on me all this time without my knowing it. Why? For no better reason than the pure pleasure of aggravating me.

When I opened the door, the cats came yowling, thinking I was going to feed them, so that I nearly broke my neck trying to get down the rickety stairs. Then I had to stop at the road to shoo the dog back. A car tooted, and someone waved. It took me a second to recognize who it was: the priest's housekeeper, driving his big brown sedan with him sitting beside her. And there I stood, in my old housedress with the holes and stains on a Sunday afternoon, shooing the dog away from the road with one hand and holding up the claw hammer with the other to wave hello to the priest.

The emptiness came over me suddenly, and I got lost in it. It was because I was crossing over to Ruby's again, with the deserted road and the broken-down farm, everything, reminding me of all that I had lost.

So it seemed fitting that I would climb her steps and try her door, only to find it bolted from the inside. I knocked, with no answer, knocked again, and finally let loose with the hammer, nearly splintering the wood.

"What's the matter, is it locked?" she asked, breathless.

She didn't wait for an answer. She flittered around, knocking over a framed photograph of some long-dead relatives from the shelf by the door; then she stooped to pick it up and set it back, asking me if I knew who they were and if I'd ever seen it before.

"Everytime I come here you show it to me," I told her, weary already.

She laughed. "Boy, what a memory you have. Your kids must take after you. Of course, Leonard's smart, too. Our whole family is smart."

Carl called from the kitchen, "Who is it, Ruby?"

"Come in, come in," she shouted, waving and fidgeting and bustling, so that I felt like I was caught up in the giant corn combine.

Carl sat in his rocking chair by the stove. He snorted when he saw me. "Well, it's the *Stranger* come to visit," he said. He laughed and rocked faster.

I was surprised at how everything looked the same: the counter cluttered with dead geranium plants she'd brought up from the cellar, stacks of magazines, tin cans, a broken radio; the table cluttered with papers and books, her purse, a bowl of leaky pens and rubber bands; knick-knacks crammed everywhere; greeting cards from the last two holidays scotch-taped to one wall; a pan of cooked food on the stove and dishes in the sink. And then there was the smell, the closed, stale smell of food and of *them*; and the heat, as if even on this warm day she had the furnace blasting.

"Stop, Carl," Ruby said. "Watch out for the wall."

"I'm not hurting anything," he said, and he kept rocking.

She reached out to slow him down, and that's when I noticed. She held her right arm down at her side. The hand was inside an old mayonnaise jar.

I took a seat at the table and lay the hammer in front of me, on top of a pile of opened mail and some newspaper clippings. So, I thought to myself, I am back in Ruby Mondo's house, all right. I folded my hands and looked at her, waiting to see what she'd say.

She turned to the stove and lit a burner. "How about some tea?"

"You know I don't drink tea," I told her.

"Maybe if you tasted it you'd like it. How would you know if you never tried?"

"Did you want something?" I asked.

She gave me a look like she didn't understand.

"You called me over here," I said, my eye on that jar.

"Oh. I did, didn't I?" She gave a little laugh, like she was embarrassed, which it looked to me she had good reason to be.

And then while the tea heated up, she busied herself at the sink, running water, knocking over a geranium and setting it right, and I could see it was all going to be up to me.

So I finally said to her, "How can you be canning so early in the year?"

"Canning? Why, I haven't been canning." She sounded indignant.

Carl started up with the rocking again. "Miss Ruby's got her hand stuck in a jar."

"It's stuck?" I asked. I could see darn well that it was.

Anyone else would have found it funny. Anyone who hadn't lived all these years with Ruby Mondo, that is, with one thing after another like this, day in and day out, and her supposed to be so smart, able to think things through.

She wouldn't say it was stuck. "I can't seem to get my hand out" was as much as she'd admit. "I thought you could break it for me. With the hammer."

I looked at her a minute, thinking, "There's a lot more than that jar this hammer could break about now."

I went over to get a closer look. When I lifted the jar, Ruby went quiet for the second time in one day. She turned her face to the side, like I was looking at something private on her.

"Did you try putting oil on it?" I asked, my voice gruff. I could see the hand was dry as a dog bone and red, from trying to pull it out. It looked pitiful, closed up like that.

"Oil?" she murmured. She gazed off at the kitchen window a minute like she was going someplace in her head. "By golly, that's right." She jumped up and shuffled through the heap of papers near the phone. "This is what I wanted to show you." She held out a magazine article to me, as if this was the real reason she'd called me over and it had just come back to her.

The article was about porpoises, how smart they were and how they could even talk.

"Isn't language fascinating?" she said. "Thousands of different languages the world over and most people are lucky if they know only one or two. Just think, though, God understands them all." A moment later she added, "But of course, why wouldn't He?"

I used to tell Len her mind worked like the algebra she taught: If you didn't understand the formulas, none of it made sense. I never took algebra in school. I didn't know the first thing about it.

"Shall we get this over with?" I said.

I took her bottle of cooking oil down from the cupboard, and a dish towel, and had her sit at the table. "If you were able to get your hand in this jar," I told her, "you should be able to get it out."

"You gotta use a shoehorn," Carl said. He snorted and laughed.

"That's for shoes, Carl," Ruby told him.

"I know it," he said, and he laughed again.

I worked the oil around her wrist while her free hand went scrabbling through the junk on her table the way her mind ran from one topic to another. "Inventors," she said. She fished out a metal paper clip and held it up for me to see. "It takes a genius to think up something like this."

The oil wasn't working. "Should I try some soap?" I said. "Warm soapy water?"

She shrugged. "Oh, do what you like." This was her hand we were talking about, her hand I was working on.

"That Leonardo da Vinci," she said. "He's another one." She shook her head over the thought of him. "Of course, we're all special," she said. "We've all been put here for a reason, that's not news."

I didn't need one of her geniuses to figure out the only thing I'd been put here for: cleaning up other people's messes.

"If you'd stop moving around so much," I told her, "maybe I could get this hand out."

I worked some dish soap around her wrist, though it didn't do any good.

"Why didn't you say something if I was moving too much?"

"I'm saying something."

She gave me an odd look, then laughed.

"Look here. Maybe you can figure this out," she said. "Get your mind on a more positive note." She held up a newspaper clipping of names for me to read. She'd cut the article away so there was no heading, no story, nothing except names.

"What is this?" I said. "Who are they?"

"I thought you knew."

"I don't know," I told her. She does that. Saves things, then forgets what they are. Then she expects me to know what her junk is about. It was like she stored up everything for me, just waiting so she could dump it all out. She couldn't talk about these foolish things with anyone else.

"I have no idea what this is," I told her. "These names mean nothing to me."

"Well you don't have to get cross."

I rapped my knuckles hard against the jar, to change the subject before she had me packing my bags for the same rest home she should have put Carl in.

"Is there a purpose to this?" I said. "Or did you just put your hand in here for something to do?"

She shrugged, and the movement sent a few greeting cards to the floor. "I was in a hurry, that's all. Never do anything in a hurry or you'll regret it, don't they always say that?"

I made a move to pick up the cards, then decided to heck with them.

"I thought I'd be smart, see?" she said. "And get to the bank before it closed."

The minute she let the words out, her face bloomed scarlet, right under my eyes, like one of those high-speed films that shows a rosebud opening.

I stopped what I was doing. "The bank?" I said. "You mean Friday? You've had your hand in this jar since Friday?"

She gave me a look that reminded me of our dog, the time we found him caught in a muskrat trap.

I got some satisfaction, then. I pictured her going to bed like that, tucking the jar under the covers, trying to cook, trying to eat, trying to shave Carl, all with her left hand while the other was closed up in that jar. And then, for once, I almost felt like laughing. Almost, but not quite.

When it passed, I looked at her, and what I saw was a wisp of smoke. That smoke was my life and the lives of my kids.

I picked up the hammer and felt its weight, considering.

"This won't work," I told her, and I put the hammer back down. "You'll get cut."

"What's a little cut? It'll heal."

I eyed her. Then I thought, All right. If that's what you want. Just remember you asked for it.

She looked over at the hammer, like she knew what I was thinking.

"Look," she said, a little too cheerfully, "I bet you can't figure this out." She dug out another article. "Here's a story about two brothers. The oldest boy—he's a man now—is only ten years younger than his mother. And he wasn't adopted. Now how can that be?"

"I haven't the foggiest idea," I told her.

"Try," she said.

"Oh, Ruby, please."

"He was in a foster home," she said. "It was his foster mother. Of course, it's nothing new. Even Moses had a foster mother, everybody knows that. You don't just find a baby floating in the bulrushes and think it doesn't belong to somebody."

And I thought, for this I came to Len and had four kids.

"But what a so-and-so that pharoah must have been," she was saying. "Didn't he think it was funny that his daughter had a baby when she wasn't even expecting one?"

Everything belonged to her. Everything had a story behind it, a history, a whole thread of connections that somehow related to her personally, as if she was involved in every single event that had ever happened or would happen, and there was no such thing as time. No wonder I couldn't figure which of them was the battier, Carl or her.

I looked over at him. He wore his cowboy shirt tucked into his dungarees, and his fat stomach strained against the belt. He didn't look that much off, but his mind just wasn't right. He sat watching us, content as pie. I wondered what she saw when she looked at Carl, how she imagined him. Her *brother*.

"Of course, when you think about it," she said, "we're all foster children. That's nothing new."

Her words trailed off as I went for some old newspapers under her TV stand.

She gave the papers an anxious look. "I hope there's nothing in there I wanted to save," she said.

I dropped the stack on the table. "Shall I cut out some names for you?"

"I can call somebody if you've got work to do," she told me. "I don't want to keep you if you're not feeling up to snuff."

We both knew she didn't have anyone else to call. "I'm going to get this over with," I told her.

"I would've done it myself, but I didn't have a hammer," she said. "Of course, I could have used a rock. But if something happened—"

What she meant was if she cut herself. What if she landed in a hospital—or worse. What about *Carl* was what she meant.

"But by gosh, I'm lucky to have you next door," she said, and she knocked on the wood of the table leg for superstition's sake. "Thank goodness I've got you."

It threw me for a loop. She'd never said a word to let on I meant anything to her—or that she even noticed the things I did for her. Then I got worried, that she was counting on me to take over if anything happened.

"But you're too serious," she said. "You should have come to our party, that would've cheered you up."

I thought, She has some nerve thinking I need cheering up, when if it wasn't for her—

"All your kids were here. Of course, Leonard was working. He's another one, always working."

That stopped me. "The kids?" I said. "What are you talking about?"

"It wasn't exactly a party. I played the piano and we sang songs."

Carl moved into high gear with the rocker and started singing, *"Home, home on the range."*

"That's right, Carl," she said. *"Where the deer and the antelope play.* Oh well, this was back before Easter. Right before your daughter went away." She drummed her fingers on the table and nodded her head to the tune that was in there. "Where would we be without music? It's a universal language, did you know that?"

The only time the kids went over that I knew of was when they wanted to tease Carl and Ruby, get them going; and then it was just the two who were speaking to each other who went. I couldn't see all four of them putting aside their grudges long enough to go visiting, much less to sing songs together.

"Of course, mathematics is another universal language," Ruby said. "There are probably others, too, if we just stop to think about it." Her face went serious as she thought about it. Then she said, "It took a lot of planning to pitch in and have that reproduction made and keep it all a surprise."

I didn't know what she was talking about, as usual. "Reproduction?" I asked her.

"That your kids gave me, of Ma and Pa's wedding picture."

Now it was my turn to forget the reason I was in her house. I dropped the hand. "My kids came over and gave you a picture?" Even as I was saying the words it came to me that she'd been talking about wanting a copy of that wedding photograph since I'd known her.

I hadn't heard a word about the reproduction. I didn't know anything about any of it.

"Of course, your oldest girl was behind it all," Ruby said. "It was her idea. But where'd they get that frame?"

My girl? I thought. And just like that, Ruby had conjured her up for me, and I stood there dumbfounded by what I saw. But then a new kind of panic hit me, because I realized who else but Ruby Mondo would go slogging through the bulrushes of life and stumble upon my babies?

"I hope the frame doesn't belong to anybody," Ruby said, and she made a move to get up.

I put my hand on the jar and held her to the table.

"Well, by golly, you're right," she said. "We can look at it anytime. Always take care of the business at hand."

I spread newspapers over the junk on her table, so she wouldn't have broken glass in everything. Maybe her cut would heal, but mine refused. It had been eating at me all these years: what I had done to my kids on account of her. Because once I found out what I had gotten myself into by marrying the three of them—Len, Carl, and Ruby—it was more than I could take. I left them all to fight it out on their own, with a sink full of dirty dishes, and the washing machine hose broken and spilling water onto the floor, the baby crying because he'd dropped his plastic soldier man down the heat register, the cats and dogs and Ruby and Carl tracking in dirt, everybody underfoot and squabbling for attention, a house full of mess and noise and commotion. My body stayed behind, though, so it looked like I was there, but I wasn't.

They learned that much from me—how to keep your own flesh and blood from knowing you.

I spotted a stack of rolled nickels, over near the edge of her table, half-buried under papers. One roll was open. She must have been getting them ready to take to the bank for deposit when her money jar decided to play a trick on her.

Right then it played a trick on me, too. I looked at it and saw my daughter sitting on the bus again, all closed up, her hand raised like a sign, calling me to her, keeping me away.

I lifted Ruby's wrist, to put it on the newspapers, and the picture disappeared. "You've got to stay still, now," I told her.

Her skin looked like it would crack if you so much as breathed on it. But it was soft as a baby's.

And there I stood, working over my own again, to get the burdock or bubble gum out of their hair, or a thumb into the thumbhole of a mitten, while they jiggled their legs and touched things and gabbed on with whatever popped into their heads, and me saying, "Mm-hmm. Stay still, now."

Ruby started off on some story about a boy she'd had in school who'd invented windshield wipers, but nobody knew about it, nobody gave him credit.

I picked up the hammer and touched it to the jar. Her

hand lay still under the glass, like something else—one more thing I didn't know anything about.

"You've got to hit harder than that," Ruby said. "You're just tapping it."

Her voice brought me back around.

I raised the hammer to Ruby Mondo while she sat with her eyes glued to that jar, like somebody in a fever, waiting for me to set her free. I tapped the jar again, and the sound rattled right through me.

"You've got to hit harder," Ruby said. "Hit it."

Carl thumped the wall with the rocking chair. "Ruby's got her hand stuck in a jar," he sang.

"Harder," I heard her say. And then I shut my eyes, and everything broke loose at last.

Carl shrieked, laughed. I could hear the pieces showering to the floor.

I thought I had smashed her hand with the hammer. I thought the glass had gone all over, that I'd driven it deep into her flesh and caused damage.

And right then it came to me: I was the one person in this whole damn town who Ruby Mondo considered her friend.

"See?" Ruby said. "That was nothing. That's all it took."

I opened my eyes and she sat beneath me, whole.

I took a seat across from her, the pile of broken glass between us.

"Now I'll just clean this up and get back to business as usual," she said, wiping her hands on the dish towel. She started folding in the edges of the newspaper.

"Wait," I said, reaching my hand out. I needed things to be still for a minute.

"Oh, look," she said.

And there it was, the red trickling down my own fingers, though I hadn't felt it.

I drew my hand back and sucked on the finger, and as soon as I did it started stinging. I took the Kleenex from my sleeve and wrapped the finger while Ruby jumped up to search through her cupboards for Band-Aids. "It's okay," I told her. "I don't need anything." But she kept rummaging.

I sat back and pressed the Kleenex tighter while I watched her bustle out of the room, then back in, then open a drawer, a cupboard, pull things out, root around. There was no stopping her.

And there I was, come full circle, right back to the kind of foolishness that drove me away, that I could not get free from: Ruby blind to the commotion she churned up, me broken and bleeding from it.

I caught sight of a nickel on the floor, just underneath the edge of the stove. The last nickel she'd been trying to retrieve, to fill the roll.

It seemed par for the course, God giving me my due like that, calling me there for the very one I blamed for losing the others, calling me back into her house for a lousy five-cent piece and a stinking mayonnaise jar.

And I saw right then and there what I should have seen years ago: that I would either have to yield, or do battle the rest of my life.

But I did not want her. I did not want that sixty-two-year-old child, and yet I had her.

She reached for my hand, to see how bad the cut was, and her reaching threw me off. I tried to pull away, but she held on.

She turned my hand over, like a gypsy palm reader looking for meaning in the scars of my life.

"Just a scratch," she said. "It's nothing."

Nothing, I thought. It's nothing, and the feelings rose up in me. But before I could say anything she pointed to some dirt on the floor, from when she'd knocked over the geranium, and she went for the broom.

She took big, choppy sweeps, dipping from the waist with each swing, so she looked more like she was hoeing weeds than sweeping a floor. Within seconds the handle of the broom tangled with her telephone cord and sent the receiver flying.

"Alexander Graham Bell!" she said. "Who would've thought a voice could travel thousands of miles over a tiny piece of wire? See what you can come up with if you put your mind to it?" She left the receiver dangling while she swept.

Maybe I was in shock from losing blood, though I hadn't lost any to speak of, not that showed anyway. But I worried about that phone, what would happen if someone tried to call right then. I wanted to get up and set it right, but my body felt like a sack filled with rocks.

"They give him all the credit," she went on, "but you know it was some German man who got the ball rolling. And who knows who else before that? Who knows how far back it goes?"

I watched her and I thought, Don't ask me how far back it goes. I can't even figure how I got here today.

"Look," she said. "Now where do you suppose this came from?" She swept out the nickel and dusted it on her sleeve. "This must be my lucky day." She dropped the nickel in her dress pocket and went on sweeping. It looked like she planned to do the whole floor now that she'd started. "Remember nickelodeons?" she said.

So Ruby Mondo had herself a friend—who didn't even know she was a friend and didn't want to be one anyway. But why her? I was asking myself. Why not somebody who could do for *me,* who could give me something in return? Besides the gray hair and varicose veins, that is.

"You never hear about nickelodeons anymore," she said.

I watched her push at the pile of dirt, making it go here and there, but not really paying any mind to where she moved it. What if my life had nothing to do with me or Len or the kids? I thought. What if it was something else altogether, something I didn't know anything about?

I felt my knees buckle right there in the chair, and I went stumbling down a steep embankment. When I hit bottom something swept over me. It pushed me under and carried me along to some cool, deep place. But as quick as it took me it flung me out again, and I came up breathing air.

I looked at her and I thought, I've got four kids, strangers or not. Maybe those invisible threads Ruby saw that connected all things and brought them back home would work for my kids, too. Maybe they were working already.

"Just like the old Victrolas," she was saying. "You never hear about them, either. But we wouldn't be where we are today without them, would we?"

She stopped sweeping and bent over to pick up a piece of glass. She held it up to show me, and winked. Then she dropped it and went back to pushing the broom, her face bright with whatever was tumbling through her mind.

I shook my head. "I guess we wouldn't," I said.

I had four kids of my own, that was, and two more by default.

And I had a head that was swimming with all the mysteries and inventions of the everyday world. Things that were right there for me to see. Things that belonged to me.

UNDERGROUND
RAILROAD

This is the only thing I know how to do: work on the dirt bike Cardamon sold me for ten bucks, which I only paid him five and he keeps waiting for the other five. "A boy like you," he says, trying to put his hand on me. "It don't have to be money." But I never let him. I got a can of kerosene, trying to wash out the rust parts to see if maybe then I can get the engine to crank for even one blasted second, with Maude sitting on the tree stump watching me the whole time not saying a word because I told her soon as it runs I'm giving you a ride and maybe we're not never coming back. So she waits for it to start, sitting there with the sun burning a hole in her head, and the door locked on us by the one that calls herself our mother, as if we wanted to be inside there with her anyway. Not even for Cardamon's five dollars.

When I hear the car coming up the road about half a mile away without a muffler I get the wire brush and go at the crank chain with it. I don't look at Maude, but I know she's waiting to see if I'll say something when Cardamon lets Pa out. The car sounds bad, like maybe he let some midget loose under the hood with a sledgehammer and when he stops to let the old man out I keep working. But then Cardamon blows his horn so I have to raise my head and nod, though I don't have to see him, even if my head is pointing that way. He pulls out, like the Fourth of July.

I can see by the way Pa walks that he is wore out worse than ever, which he says is because of us not his job. He takes slow steps to the house and I keep my head down and watch his black lunch pail bob each step he takes.

"Maude," he says, too tired to sound mad. "What I tell you about these damn crates?"

She swings her legs on the tree stump and can't say nothing. She made it herself, a playhouse from crates from the barn, and now she's got to bust it down but she won't. She took one wall and left the rest.

"It's a goddamn junkyard here," he says. We watch him reach for the door and just when I stand up to see what he will do I hear the hook get undone, so when he pulls the door it opens. Nobody is there.

We are behind him now, me and Maude, not because we want to go in there but to see if what our mother done is really done and to see what will happen now.

She is not even in the kitchen when we go in there. Sometimes it is like a dream when something happens. You go away and come back and there somebody is boiling a pot of coffee or there somebody is hammering a loose board on the step or else the room is peaceful with the sunlight and the jar of wilted daisies on the table and maybe nothing really happened, you think, maybe it was all just a dream.

He turns and says, "What the hell you two following me like puppy dogs for, don't you got nothing better to do?" But he stops a minute and his face goes funny when he sees us staring at him, like already he knows, but he doesn't know what.

And then a strange thing happens, he tries to turn his head to look at the parlor door where she's inside sitting yet he can't let go looking at us. So his head can't move and he can't move and for a minute all three of us are stuck like that. And then at last he breaks free and walks right through that black hole of a doorway and I wonder did he notice everything that's *not* there: supper not cooking, the TV not blasting, Martha not fussing to be fed or have her diaper changed? Because everything is dead still like nobody ever lived in this house.

I follow him to the parlor door and I stop there and look in and feel Maude behind me, her hair brushing my arm. The TV is going, just the picture with no sound, and she is sitting there watching it like that and the shades are pulled. Halfway into the room he stops and looks at her but she don't look back or move a muscle or act like she notices anybody is there.

He stands like that a long time. A comedy show is on the TV, soldiers riding horses and one man falls off and can't pick up his hat, the horse keeps stepping on it. Then finally Pa says, "What's going on?"

She watches the TV, with her big round face and her gray hair coming out of the ponytail, just sitting there a big heavy lump. Then she says, "I had to take some aspirins," like she's talking to the lady on the television commercial now who is frosting a cake and cutting a big slice and handing it to whoever is watching.

"Aspirins," he says, like it's a word he never heard before. He looks around at us, then back at her and he waits while something tries to sink in.

"Why you got that thing on like that?" he says. And then he waits a minute more and then his voice gets louder, but not much. "You tell me what happened," he says.

"I had to have a break," she says.

He goes over and shuts off the TV and puts a shade up so there's some light and now I can see her face, her eyes pushed in there like you pushed your thumbs into a pile of dough, looking at the TV screen with nothing on it. She stares so hard at the TV while he's looking at her that her head wobbles. I feel Maude breathing against my arm.

He stands there looking at her like he's asking her everything in the world without saying a word. He puts his hand up through his hair and turns half away, like he might start to do a dance but then decides not to. He turns back and looks at her and then at us watching from the doorway.

"Go outside," he says, and we don't move. "Git," he tells us. I take a step back and bump into Maude. We stay there.

"You tell me," he says to her, like he will bust into tears over her.

"I had to have a break," she tells him, looking at that empty television set.

He watches her a minute. "I could of give you one hell of a break a long time ago," he says.

"I wish't I had something," she says.

"You tell me," he says to her.

"It don't never let up," she says. "It's all I ever hear is fussing and crying. It don't never let up."

She's sitting there talking like one of those dead people on the late movie that's got all the blood drained out of them, and I'm thinking, Why don't he ask her why it's let up now? Why don't he say something about right now when it's never before been stone quiet in this house at suppertime?

"I thought you was done with this," he says, that choking sound in his voice, though maybe he don't even know yet what he's talking about. "I thought things was changed."

I look at her and think, You ain't my mother. I got none. And if he's my real pa, maybe that's a mistake too. All I got that's real is a sister, Maude. I had four sisters in my life but Maude is the only one alive. And then I touch her like by accident just to feel her there behind me and I can hear her breathing. I will take that bike and go. And if it won't start I will walk if I have to and I will take her because she is my sister.

Then he goes around putting up the other shades like if there's more light it'll just be a dream to him too and he can wake up.

"What the hell these shades down for?" he says. "And that TV? You crazy after all?"

He goes at the last shade like he is in a fight and the whole thing comes ripping down and clatters to the floor. He turns to her like he will break something.

"You better talk," he says, but his voice is even. "You better tell me something."

In the light she looks like a fat teenage girl but she is almost forty. And he looks like a sick old man—tall and skinny and hopeless, and too broke down for words.

"I can't move," she moans. "I'm like paralyzed."

"Goddamn," he says. "I can't ask you no more."

"It don't stop," she says. "I been telling you. I'm always telling you. They driving me this way."

"What?" he says. "What?"

"That baby won't let up."

But she's let up now, I want to say. Why don't you ask her why she's let up now?

"It's her earache," he says. "She's sick."

And then she turns her head and looks direct at him for the first time and I see those two places where the thumbs pushed down into the dough, but there's nothing there. "She's sick," she says, the words coming out of her like bubbles come out of somebody that's under water.

"Why didn't you say so?" he says. "Why the Christ hell didn't you say so?" and he sounds like he could dance all night from the relief of it. "I'll take her to the doctor."

"You got to take her somewhere," she tells him.

He turns to me and tells me, "You go over to Cardamon's, tell him we need a ride."

It's like a knife in me, to think of going there, with him always trying to touch me, after me to do things. But then it passes, and I lean back into Maude's arm and stay put.

"Them doctors don't do nothing," she says.

"Go tell Cardamon," he says to me.

"She's bad," she tells him. "You got to take her somewhere. Them doctors don't do nothing."

"Git," he tells me.

"Don't," she says then to him. "It's nobody's business."

He's still trying to act like he don't know what

he knows. But then she says that and he has to stop.

I look around at Maude and she is staring right at her, but her face is all easy like she could be looking out the window watching it rain.

"It hurts me inside my heart," she moans, and I look back at her. She puts her hand there where her heart is supposed to be. "Don't let nobody know," she says. "I been telling you," she says to him.

And then his face goes, like it's an egg and somebody cracked it hard against the side of a frying pan and it just breaks open.

I feel Maude take a step back.

He drops down on his knees on the floor in front of her.

"You got to stand by me," she says.

I look at her and think, If I had a shotgun I would kill you. I would kill him, too, on his knees like that. If I had a shotgun and that bike worked I would get out of here so fast I wouldn't even take a breath of air.

"God Jesus," he says into his hands.

"Don't forsake me," she says. "Everybody is always forsake me."

"I thought you was done with this."

"I love you so bad," she says.

If I had a shotgun, I think.

"Don't tell me this," he says. He looks up out of his hands at her. "I can't do no more." He looks at his hands, like his face left something there for him to see, then looks back at her. "I can't," he says. "I can't no more for you."

"Don't forsake me," she says.

"Where is she?" he says, like he's choking on the words.

"It never lets up," she says.

"Where?" he says.

"On the bed," she tells him. "She won't let up."

He is holding his stomach like he will break in two if he lets go.

"You got to take her somewhere," she says. "Don't get Cardamon. It's nobody's business."

Inside me it's like cinder blocks stacking up in my legs all the way to my stomach, each one telling me, What was done is really done. At night I stay awake and listen to hear if she's coming into my bedroom after me because you never know when. But I could fight her. Even if she sneaked up I would be ready, I would be awake and I would fight her. And the cinder blocks stack higher, up to my chest now.

I back up more and touch Maude. I would die if she ever laid a hand to Maude, I think.

He stands up, staggering like a deer that's been shot but is still trying to run.

"You got to take her somewhere," she says. "Don't forsake me."

He stumbles for the kitchen door and we jump out away into the kitchen and he goes past us, moving his arms like a drowning man trying to come up for air. And then he's gone down the hallway and I hear the door open down there and everything stops.

Maude gives me a look that cuts deep. She is so cool and far away, like it don't even touch her, and it scares me worse almost than what's done.

We hear him moving in the bedroom, then everything is dead still for a long time. Maude is looking at me in that cool way that fills me with shame that I am weak and helpless and it is all my fault for doing nothing. I can see into the parlor the ripped shade on the floor and the TV shut off and I feel her sitting in there, a fat pile of dough it makes me sick to think of.

Then like out of a dream Pa says my name from down the hall in that bedroom, "Wesley."

I don't answer.

"Wesley," he says again. I don't know what it is he wants and I don't want to know. I take Maude's arm and I pull her outside and she comes.

That broken piece of junk Cardamon sold me is parked over by the stump, the kerosene can and rusted parts laying all over. We move down the steps and go stand near that mess I been working on all these days and I try to think if there's anybody would buy it from me for parts.

"It ain't going to run," Maude says, matter-of-fact, like she's known it all along.

The door opens and we turn to see him standing there. I can't move or talk with fear of it.

"Go get me—in the barn," he says, and I tell him, so he won't say no more, "I'll go get Cardamon."

"Never mind Cardamon," he says.

But I start for the road. "I'll tell him come help," I say.

"Don't you go after Cardamon, goddamnit," he tells me.

"Maude," I say, and she doesn't move.

"Get back here," he tells me.

"Maude," I say.

"Get back here," he says.

And then I go back as far as Maude and I reach for her and we start running. But when we get to the road we turn toward town, not toward Cardamon's.

"What the hell you think you're doing?" he yells after us. "Get back here," he says, "goddamnit, or we'll all end up in hell."

*   *   *

It's warm and still where we pull off into the bushes and crouch down to wait. We can still hear him yelling after us a ways down.

"Where we going?" Maude says.

"Shh," I tell her, putting my hand up to her mouth. "I got to think."

But all I think is crazy thoughts, like how about if we sneak over to Cardamon's and hide in the backseat of his car with a blanket over us so after he drives to work in the morning we can get out and go someplace, like neither him nor Pa would notice a blanket with the two of us under it. Or maybe steal his car and go, which is maybe not so crazy except it's so loud you can hear it a mile away. Or walk to town and go find a sheriff or somebody which is the craziest idea of all, since they would lock me up in a jail and put Maude in another one and the rest of our lives we would never lay eyes on each other again.

She watches me a long time squatting there, waiting for me to say something that will change every minute of our lives so far. But I got nothing like that in me.

I hear Pa moving around back by the house, hollering for us, and she is watching me.

"Don't worry," I say. "We ain't going back there."

"Where we going?"

"Someplace," I say. "I got to think." But I got no idea, nothing, like we'll just stay crouched in them bushes forever.

Her eyes glaze over at me and she looks like she will spit that I got no answers, and I blurt out the words like they come flying from a slingshot. "We going to that old lady in the hills."

She stares at me like I'm one of them people at church that puts their hands in the air and babbles out tongues, then faints dead away. "The one that come that time with her husband to buy the chickens," I tell her. "And she gave you a quarter."

"Why we going there?" Maude says. "We don't know that lady."

We don't know nobody, I could tell her but don't. Instead I say, "You got a better idea?" and she gets that face on her again.

But I would have Maude spit on me, I would have her do anything because all I can think is we got a sister at home laying dead and here we have left and are crouching in the bushes talking and who knows it could be us there. And all my insides fill up with them cinder blocks again.

"You don't even know where in them hills," Maude says.

"I been there," I say, and it's true, with Cardamon riding me in his car, but I'm not sure the road and it must be three, four miles at least anyways.

"We going to walk all the way up into them hills?" she says. "We going to walk all the way there with no food or nothing?"

Pa is quiet now and we stop and listen and I don't know if he's quiet because he's taking Martha somewhere or because he's coming after us.

I motion Maude and we scat across the road and into the woods on the other side and head kitty-corner through them over to Oxbow Road. There's a little creek not far before we reach the road, little enough to jump over, and I tell her drink since we been burning in the sun all day.

But she won't. "Cow's gone the bathroom in there," she says.

I'm cupping my hands there, drinking. "They ain't no cows nowhere around here," I tell her. "You drink now or you gonna dry up and die." She looks at me a long time when I say that, then she gets down and cups her hands and drinks.

All I know is to head up the Oxbow because it goes to the hills and hope to God for the right road.

"We got to turn at the place that's got all them dogs," I tell Maude. "I know that much."

We walk up the steep hill, on the side of the road, with no cars coming, and the birds calling off in the trees. And I'm thinking, what's her name, because I know it and heard it lots of times, she's the one that raises flowers to sell and she's so old they say maybe she was the first person ever lived in this county, before there was even a town. Sawyer, Snyder, I'm thinking. Putnam, Pullman, but nothing sounds right.

The road is getting steeper and it's hard to climb, if you look back you can see everything. And when we reach the top we turn to look and I point to the lake and the town way down in there and all the fields with small dots of cows. "You said there wasn't any cows," she says.

"Must be new," I tell her, like I been there lots of times and know what I'm talking about and then I get sick with myself, sounding just like Pa, lying, and I would want shoot myself first before I ever got to be like him.

The road evens out for a little while, and there's fields on one side, with a tractor off in one field chugging up the rows spraying crops. A woodchuck stands up ahead of us near the road and looks at us, then dives into the weeds, its fur rippling like water on its back.

"What you think he's going to do with her?" Maude asks me.

It makes me sick to think, but I can't stop thinking anyway, all the time we been going, all day working on that dirt bike, every minute since she locked the door, all the time I haven't been saying a word about it.

"Will he take her to the hospital?" Maude says.

"What for?" I say.

"Will they go to jail?" she says. "Will they put them in the electric chair?" And that's the first I know that she really knows the all of it, because up till now our baby could have been sick like they said about the other two, who they said died in their sleep. But not how they think, I could've told them.

"I hope they put them in the electric chair," Maude says. I look at her my sister swinging her arms and walking on the side of the road like some young girl that lived up in them hills talking about going to the county fair or berry picking and it makes me go cold.

I could curse myself, I could beat my own self black and blue for not knowing how to fix that bike or not having the guts to steal Cardamon's car or, worse, for not getting out and taking both of them with me and it may as well have been me that done it, and I can't bear it, I can't bear to think that way, but it won't stop.

"The next house we pass," I tell her, "I'm stealing their car if they got one. I'm getting me some money and driving us to Florida."

She looks like I just told her Santa Claus is here and she don't know if she should believe me or not. "They got coconut trees there," she says. "I want to see a coconut tree."

"You look see if there's a car I can steal," I tell her.

But when we pass the farm I am too scared and ashamed of it and we don't say nothing, we just keep our eyes on the big old brown car parked by the road with no people around, not even a dog, and we just keep walking.

Pretty soon there's a road up ahead, with a faded sign with no words left on it and she looks at me to see what I will do.

"This ain't the one," I say, but I'm not sure anymore, and we keep going.

I watch her trudge along, looking like she will go anywhere and not even care how long it takes. She is a little girl, but she will go anywhere if I tell her it's okay and then that awful feeling comes back, that I am supposed to know things and I am supposed to keep them from getting hurt, but I don't know nothing and they are hurt to death anyway.

A car comes up the hill behind us and slows down and looks. It's a boy with his long hair combed back with his sleeves rolled up and his skinny arm dangling a cigarette butt out the window, and music playing on the radio. He scowls like he's pretending he wasn't looking at us and speeds off straight ahead. He flicks the butt out the window into the road and it's out by the time we get there.

Then we just walk a long time without talking.

When I look up, there's that pen up ahead on the corner where they keep all them dogs.

"That's the road," I say. There's nothing inside the pen but tall weeds and a couple plastic bowls and some worn-out spots in the weeds, with a broken-down shed on the side of the pen and a run-down house. We stop a minute and I try to think, left or right. I try to remember in the car with Cardamon, which way we come from and which way we went, and first I think it's got to be one way, but then I don't know, it seems the other.

"Don't you know where it is?" she tells me. "This ain't even the road, is it?"

Then out the blue I think of that boy and that's how I know to turn left, because he threw his cigarette that way and he is in a car speeding down the road somewhere and he is free.

"I know where I'm going," I tell her, and we go that way where I probably never been before. But at least we are going.

"I wish't I had a baloney sandwich," she says.

"Why you always talking about food?" I say, but I wish't I had something, too.

"Will they put us in jail with them?" she says.

"We ain't done nothing," I tell her, but I don't know. And it's not the police I am afraid of, because he was going to the barn not the hospital, so nobody would even know, like if a cat got run over in the road and he went to bury it. And I wonder if already he's out there coming after us, afraid what if we tell somebody.

"We ain't done nothing," I say.

"We almost there yet?" she says.

"Almost," I tell her, but I don't know nothing, just like Pa.

Up a ways a dirt road goes off to the right and the road goes up a hill just a little bit, with trees hanging over, making like a cool tunnel. It's a nice road and I turn onto it, I don't know why. The trees make everything seem darker, though it's not dark. It's like being inside some place, out of the light of day.

"It's spooky in here," Maude says. And it is, so quiet and covered that I look into the trees and wonder if they been following us, if Pa's in there right now with his eyes on us, ready to do something.

But then the trees widen out and up ahead is a house.

"It's a dead end," Maude says. We walk up to the wood fence along the road in front of the house and stop. "You took us to a dead end," she says.

The house is a plain little shack of gray boards with no paint, with a dirt path from the road to the steps. On one side the path is some tomato and cabbage plants. On the other side is flowers. Sweet peas and weeds grow tangled on the fence, and we stand there at the end of the road looking at that beat-up house.

"Them's the flowers she sells?" Maude says.

"I told you I knew how to get here," I tell her. But all I can think is this is not the place, that's not enough flowers to sell, and now we got to turn around and go back all the way down to the other road and hope it don't get dark. And I think for real this time if I see a car I will steal it.

"You going up there?" Maude says.

But I stand looking at the house, not moving, and my feet just want to lay down and not go anywhere for a long time.

"You gonna knock on the door?" she says.

"Hello," I say. "Anybody home?" But not loud enough for anybody to hear.

As soon as I say it a big dog comes pushing its way out from around the house and trots down the path to us, all the tags on its collar jangling, like it's been waiting for us to get there. It stops and shakes its big head, jangling, and looks at us like it's saying How you doing, What's new with you, a big red long-hair dog.

Maude backs up a step, he's so big. Then she says, "You could ride him. You could put a saddle on him and ride," and she touches him on the top of the head.

There's a funny sound from the side of the house, like

some kind of bird I never heard before and the dog looks, and me and Maude look. But it's not a bird, it's an old lady calling, "Here, Boy. Where are you?" in a voice I never heard nothing like before. She comes around the side of the house, walking slow and carrying a wicker basket. She strains to see us and keeps coming, saying, "Who's there? Francis Beal, did you finally come to mow my lawn?" in that voice way up high like a bird.

We don't say nothing, we just stare at her. She's tiny and shriveled up inside a blue sack of a dress, and she's wearing socks and corduroy slippers. Her hair is fluffy and jumbled like the inside of a bird's nest.

"What did you find, Boy?" she says, looking at us, and the dog jangles his chain and looks at her like he's the happiest dog that ever got born on earth.

When she's halfway to us, I see some flowers sticking out the wicker basket and all I can think is God Almighty we're here.

"You bought them chickens from us," I shout at her, like we been looking for each other our whole lives and she should run up and throw her arms around me. "We come to the right place," I tell Maude.

The old lady stops and looks at us funny. "Last week at the store?" she says.

"Down on the farm on Glass Factory Road," I tell her. "Two, three years ago."

"Only it's not a farm no more," Maude says.

"Why it's a couple of children," she says. "Two or three years ago?" and she just looks at us blank, like her whole face is under water that she is trying to see through. The lines on her face run so deep you could plant beans in them, and she is small and frail like a bird, it makes me wonder how she can even stand up.

"You say you're looking for chickens?" she says. And

then she shakes her head, looking at us like there's something pitiful in us being there.

Which there is, more than she'd ever want to know. "I'm sorry," she says. "I don't have any chickens."

I look at Maude and see her face go soft, like one by one those strings holding any kind of hope to her are snapping away.

"You say you've come all the way from Glass Factory Road?" she says, and her head shakes and then I see her arms and hands shake, too, trembling like she's so old she's coming apart. "Well I don't know where you got the idea I had chickens."

And I just stare at her, wondering how all them words can come out of somebody who looks like she's about ready to fall over any minute.

It looks like she's ready to turn around and go in the house, so I yell out to her, "We're looking for a place to stay."

That stops her. "You ran away from home," she says.

"God no," I tell her. "We're on vacation."

She starts laughing, and it sends a chill up me, sounding like a brood of pheasants calling out to each other.

"Why, you can't be a day over fourteen," she says, shaking. If she only had a collar and tags she'd be jangling like her dog.

"I'm twenty-one," I tell her, and Maude shoots me a look that could make me choke. "My sister here is eighteen."

She wobbles her head at us. "On a walking vacation from Glass Factory Road?" she says.

"We don't live there no more," I tell her. "We live in Florida. We just come back for a visit."

Then her face gets serious and it looks like those

watery eyes of hers are searching us out, trying to find the truth if they look hard enough. "You'd better go on back home," she says. She puts her hand out, and that big ox of a red dog jangles over so his head just fits under her hand. "I'm sorry I can't sell you any chickens," she says. "Or help you on your vacation."

"I don't want no damn chickens," I say to her. "Don't you know nothing?"

"We better get going now," Maude says.

"I'm going all right," I tell her. I turn around, giving the place a good looking over, but there ain't a car parked there, not a toolshed nor a blasted barn nor a garage nor nothing but a fence and a broke-down little house with a crazy old lady and a dumb-ox dog.

"We got to walk all the way back now?" Maude says. "We got to go back there?"

"Stop railing at me, will you?" I tell her. "Can't you give me half a minute to think?" with that old lady standing there trembling all over, watching us, her hand out on the dog's head like it's the only thing keeping her from falling over.

"You said you knew where you was going," she tells me.

"Will you let up?" I say.

"You knew she was doing it," she tells me. "You could of made her stop."

"Oh God Almighty," I say to her, and she has cut me right in two so I feel like I will fall to the floor from it, like Pa.

"Do you want me to call your mother and father for you?" the lady says, and it's too much for me to take, coming from both of them like that.

And then that dumb dog trots over and noses at

Maude. "Git," I tell it. "Get the goddamn hell away from here," and Maude sticks her hand out and pats its fat head.

"Don't you talk like that," the old lady says. "You don't walk into a lady's yard and start cussing."

"Martha heard a dog barking down the road and said, 'Dog,' clear as day," Maude says.

"Don't tell me no more," I say. "Don't tell me no more about it."

"Boy," the lady says, trembling like she's gonna fall any minute now that the dog's not there holding her up, and she's nodding her head, looking at us like she's trying to see what's going on, as if it's something you can see.

"Come inside," she says, and I think she's talking to her dog. "Come use the phone and straighten this out."

"Ain't nothing to straighten," I tell her. "Ain't nothing to be done except get as far as China."

"Do you want me to call for you?" she says.

"Anyways, we ain't even got a telephone," Maude tells her.

"Oh," the lady says, like somebody just give her a little poke and she's hopping back from it.

The dog jumps up on Maude, or tries to, and she backs off and nearly falls down, he's so big.

"Boy," the lady says. "What's he doing?" she says. "He never does that."

Then it's like she gets a bright idea, just like that, and she starts wobbling worse than ever. "While you're deciding what to do," she says, "could you eat some pie?"

"We got to go," I tell her, but already my mouth is watering over from that word. I ain't tasted it in a year, maybe more.

"Pie," Maude says, real quiet, like she's in church and some holy words just come out her mouth.

The dog jangles back over to the lady, and the two of them turn and tremble into the house.

I look at Maude and she looks at me and then I don't even know what's happening, all I know is me and Maude are walking into that old lady's house.

It's dark in there, from getting late, and the sun low behind the trees and just a little window over the sink and another one facing out where there's trees and shade. She moves over near the sink, running her hands along the edge of the sink to the cupboard, and takes two dishes and pulls out half a pie from I don't know where. "I never eat pie," she says. "Mr. St. Clair from the church group brought it. He's always stopping by with something." And then she puts them two plates down on the table with big hunks of pie on them.

So we sit down and I have to lean over to see what it is, and I smell it, blackberry maybe, so sweet it hurts me. Maude hunches over hers and picks up her fork like some big spear and she is going to catch this one, this one ain't getting away. I take a bite, and it makes me go weak all over, and then that's all we do is eat, till we're down to scraping juice from the empty dishes.

I come up like from a dream and look over at the old lady sitting at the table with us now, moving her head like she's been keeping a beat to the scraping sounds. "I never did go for sweets," she says, "not even when I was little. I should just tell people I don't eat sweets, then they wouldn't give these things to me."

And I'm thinking she really is crazy, to tell people don't give her nothing sweet. Then I hear the dog drinking water, making so much noise it's like waves crashing on the rocks, and the lady says, "I didn't even offer you anything to drink with that pie." But then she don't offer anything still.

So finally Maude says, "Can I have a drink?" After some creaking and moving around the lady's up and going to the refrigerator. "I don't even think I have anything," she says. When she opens the door the light shines out and that's how I see how dark it's getting. She sticks her hand in and feels around, then pulls out a milk bottle. "I didn't think I had any," she says, and she puts it down on the table and puts a couple glasses down and says, "Can you pour for yourself?" like we're some kind of babies. We drink her milk with her standing there holding on the back of her chair watching us. Maude watches her right back while she drinks.

Finally Maude says, "Don't you have no lights in this house?"

"Oh," the lady says. "Is it too dark?" and she reaches up in the air over our heads and waves her hand around until she catches the string and pulls and the light goes on.

It's like a light flicks on inside me, too. I look at her and think, I've seen a man who was deaf and a boy with one arm but I never seen nobody that was blind. I wave my hand in the air in front of her but she doesn't look.

"Is that better?" she says.

I fling my hand right up near her face and Maude looks at me like I'm nuts, but the lady doesn't blink.

"Damn," I say.

And then, like I just won a shopping spree in a toy store I race my eyes around that room, checking how many cupboards and drawers she's got that might be holding money.

I grin at Maude and nudge her. "I told you we was going to Florida," I say. When the old lady cocks her head my way I say, "Back to Florida."

"My brother lived in Fort Lauderdale eight years,"

she says, "and I never once went to visit him. I just never wanted to. I liked staying put here."

I stand up, looking around. "You couldn't pay me to stay here," I tell her. "I'm glad we left when we did. Ain't you glad, Maude?"

"Uh-huh," she says, nodding her head and giving me a look that says What you talking about? What kind of business you thinking to do now?

"Where in Florida are you from?" the lady says.

I got my hand on one of her drawers, ready to pull it out when she says that and I stop dead in my tracks, racking my brains for the name of some town, but I don't know a one. "The Everglades," I tell her.

"Ho!" she says. Then she starts real slow and quiet with a laugh until pretty soon we got that whole brood of pheasants back in there crawing to each other.

"It's a little town nobody ever heard of," I tell her, and I take my hand off the drawer and look around the room. She's sitting at the end of the table, trembling her head with her shriveled hands fidgeting on the table. "It's mostly colored people live there," I say, and she trembles her head, smiling. Maude sits there shaking her head at me like I am the sorriest person she has ever laid eyes on.

"I've met some colored people from Florida," the old lady says, and I'm thinking, God Almighty, ain't she got a purse somewhere that I can just nab it and hightail out of there?

"They came up on the railroad," the lady says. "A few settled here. Most were from Georgia and Alabama, though." Her head's nodding all over and she's smiling away. "My great-grandfather worked for the railroad. Did you know it came right through here? Did you know this is historical land that you're on?"

Maybe that's why she's not locked up, I'm thinking. One minute she's giving you a piece of pie like she's all right. Then she starts talking like that, but she keeps fooling you with it. I open a cupboard door and peek in but it's only cans of soup and other such junk in there.

"Did you want something else?" she says.

I nearly jump out of my skin and catch myself from slamming the door shut. I stare hard at her trying to figure out if she really can see. But those eyes are all watery and funny-looking and she sits there wobbling like she's waiting for a parade to come.

"There ain't no train up in these hills," Maude says.

The old lady grins at her, like Maude just said something too smart for words. "Of course it's not here anymore," she says.

I see through the door what's got to be her bedroom and I wonder how I'm gonna get in there to look around without starting a ruckus.

She's off smiling, nodding her head and blinking her eyes at something from a long time ago. "I'm proud my family was a part of it," she says.

"We got a cousin worked for the railroad," Maude tells her, "cutting weeds along the tracks."

The old lady laughs. "I'm talking about the underground railroad," she says.

I'm heading for the bedroom, quiet, so she don't hear me, trying to see around the doorway if there's a purse or anything worth some money in there.

"It goes through tunnels?" Maude says.

"No," the old lady says so sharp and sudden I think she is saying it to me, and I stop cold. Maude yawns and runs her finger down the pie plate, but there's nothing to get. Tunnels, I'm thinking. Clear from here to Florida.

The old lady looks at me like she sees me going into her bedroom, and I'm stopped there like a treed coon. I see now she knows I'm aiming to steal any good thing I can lay my hands on. "No tunnels," she says, looking at me funny, and it hits me right then the old craw's lying, scared I'm going to haul her loot down into them tunnels and disappear.

I come back slow to the table and stand next to Maude, eyeing that old lady, with her head going this way and that and everything on her a tremble.

"I been on a underground railroad once," I tell her, but I'm lying. "It was nothing," I say, and I shrug. Maude's looking at me like I just lost any little bit of sense I had left.

But then she turns back to the old lady. "Howcome it don't run here no more?"

"There's no more need," the lady says. "Thank God for that."

Now I know she's lying because people are always wanting to go places and if there was a train they could get out and not be stuck here like a burdock root in hard land.

"That little brick building where the road turns in Peterboro," the lady says. "That was one of the stops."

I look at her wondering if she's trying to throw me off or if she's so dumb she forgot she didn't want me to know. But she's not looking at me. She's sitting there smiling and wobbling her head at Maude's like it's only her and Maude in the world and she plumb forgot I was even in the room.

We could walk there in a couple hours, it's that close. We could walk there and get in them tunnels and nobody would ever know on earth what happened to us, not even Pa. Not even that one that killed my sisters. And all along I was picturing caves and rocks being the way in. I never thought of walking inside no little brick building in the middle of a town to reach them.

"We better get along now," I say to Maude. "It's getting late."

"Where to?" she says, like it never crossed her mind that we could leave that old lady's house.

"Where you think?" I tell her. "Home," I say, so the old lady won't think anything.

"Home?" Maude cries out, and I have to throw my hand up over her mouth, and then I put my finger to my lips, too, to make her see she's got to keep shut up and do what I say.

That dumb dog is laying under the table somewhere snoring, and the old lady sits there wobbling her head looking around like a chicken trying to see in the dark.

"You said we wasn't ever—" Maude says, and I clamp my hand tighter.

"We got to go back to the car," I tell her, making faces to try to make her wake up and catch on. "Back to the Everglades."

And then she just flat out starts bawling.

"Goddamnit," I say. "Why you got to start that? Goddamnit to hell," and I take my hand away and let her go at it. The dog rattles out from under the table and sticks its big square nose up on the table to see what's happening.

The old lady sits there a minute taking it in. Then she stands up slow and wobbling. Maude sits there bawling with her eyes on the old lady, watching what she's going to do. She goes to the sink, feeling around and running water, and I stand there helpless in a broken-down house on a dead-end road nowhere up in the hills. I sit back down at the table and let them cinder blocks stack up inside me again because I can't stand it no more from the weight of them.

The old lady wobbles over to Maude with a wet washrag. When Maude sees that cloth come at her she shuts up and moves to get away, but the lady plops it right on her.

"This always helped me when I was weepy," she says to Maude. "Washing my face with cool water."

Maude sits there like the bogeyman jumped out the woods and scared her out of her skin, while the old lady runs that cloth all over her face, going off into her hair and against her nose, feeling for where the face is. She puts one of them shriveled hands on Maude's shoulder to hold her steady while she rubs her face down and Maude goes stiff. "Doesn't that feel good?" the old lady says, but Maude is stiff and struck dumb from it.

"I should wash your face, too," she says to me, and I jump to.

"Don't nobody wash my face but me," I tell her. "Don't nobody better try."

She lets off with Maude, and Maude sits there blinking her eyes like she just come out of the dark and don't know where she is.

"Maybe you'd get some help if you told somebody," the lady says, wobbling her head.

I look at her wondering what it is she knows we should tell.

She goes over and drops that washrag in the sink. "A little girl like you belongs home in bed this time of night," she says. Maude sits there like a rock, with her eyes on the old lady, not saying nothing.

"Your mother and father are going to be worrying about you," she says.

"You ain't kidding," I tell her, thinking they're worrying right now are we telling somebody what's going on. And then I go creepy again, thinking of Pa outside somewhere, moving through the woods, hunting us down.

"Our mother—" Maude says, and I swing around and look at her.

"Shut up, Maude," I tell her. "Don't you say nothing." I move to get her up and get going, but she's like somebody who's drunk too much and won't budge. "We're going now," I tell her.

"They'll put her in the electric chair," Maude says.

"Shut up," I yell at her, and it's like a knife cutting me what she says. I look over at the old lady who's all trembling and a-fluster-looking.

"I hope they do," Maude says. "I hoped they put them both in."

I take Maude's arm and try to pull her from the chair. "We got to go," I tell her. "You going to get us in big trouble if you don't shut up." I yank but she still don't come.

"If something bad has happened—" that lady says.

"Every blasted thing is something bad," I tell her.

And then I don't care no more. I go open a cupboard door and start pushing things around. I take out a can of peaches.

"What are you looking for?" she says.

"I gotta find me something," I tell her.

"You ask if you want something," she tells me. "You don't go snooping in people's cupboards."

I open a drawer that's full of spoons and forks. Then I go to the bedroom.

"Come back here," she says, and she starts after me, knocking into a chair. "What are you doing?" That big ox of a dog jangles up and lumbers after her.

It's an old lady's bedroom, all dusty and still and smelling like old no-good powder. She's got a big bed with posts and a bedspread and fat pillows. There's nothing on the dresser but a doily and a dish with some dust and bobby pins in it.

The dog comes up behind me, I can feel it nosing my leg. "What do you want?" the lady says.

I open the top drawer and throw my hand in to root around, then pull it back out just as fast. The drawer is full of her underthings, all laid out in there. I close it and turn around like the breath got knocked out of me.

I blink and I'm still seeing all them white things I touched, and the hooks and snaps. Something comes up in my throat and sticks there, and now I'm stuck too, all the way inside an old lady's bedroom with her blocking the door and looking like she thinks I'm fixing to kill her.

"I ain't here to hurt you," I tell her, and it sounds funny the way it comes out, and I'm looking at her like maybe she can do something to help.

The dog's standing there, the both of them watching me.

"I got to get me and my sister out of here," I say, the words choking out of me. She just wobbles her head and moves her eyes trying to see.

"Lady," I tell her, "I got to have some money."

She looks at me relieved, like I just told her the best news of her life.

"Why didn't you say so before?" she says. "Instead of going through my things. You could have mowed my lawn."

"I'll mow it for you now," I tell her, thinking why not, for a blind lady who can't see how bad it'll look.

"It's too dark for you," she says. "Come out of my bedroom."

"I'm coming," I tell her. "But you got to move." I'm

scared she's going to grab me or do something, feeble as she is and I could knock her down if I sneezed hard. But she backs on out into the kitchen and the dog with her, and I go too.

I'm trembling almost as bad as she is from being in there. Maude gives me a scared look like she can't believe what I done and maybe the lady will call the police now.

"He didn't mean nothing," Maude says.

"Honey, it's all right," the lady tells her.

But I'm wild inside. I look to Maude and I know we got to get before something big goes wrong.

"What's happened to you?" the lady says. "What do you need money for?"

I wave my hand at her like she can see to say it don't matter, nothing don't matter. "To live," I say. "That's what for."

I put my hand on that can of peaches I took down and hold it. "Ain't nothing happened to me yet," I tell her.

"You're a good boy," she says. "I know you are."

I look at her and shake my head, lost.

And then it comes to me like a flash, that she is crazy and anything could happen. So I tell her, "I'll come back tomorrow and mow your lawn. If you pay me now."

She wobbles her head at me a long time, like if she looks hard enough she'll start to see something. Finally she says, "I'll pay you half. I'll give you one dollar now."

It feels like my stomach just sunk to the bottom of the ocean. A dollar, I want to say. What the damn good's a dollar going to do? I look over at Maude and she's got that blank face on her again, like she don't want to let herself believe any of this could turn out good.

"I'll come do it in the morning," I tell the lady.

She trembles her head and gets up. She creaks over to

the sink and pulls out a tin mop pail from underneath. Inside the pail is her pocket-book, after all the damn snooping I done and going through her bedroom dresser too. She pulls it out right in front of us and brings it back to the table.

It takes forever. She's got to sit back down and fumble to open it and then fumble to pull out her money purse and fumble to feel through that. Finally she takes a bill out and lays it on the table, a twenty-dollar bill.

Maude starts to open her mouth, but I stop her.

The old lady sits there wobbling, and I can't tell if she knows it's a twenty and she's up to something or if it's just that she can't see nothing.

I touch the money to see what she'll do, and I go weak, I never touched that much before. She sits there nodding her head and does nothing.

I look over at Maude, and then I pick up the money and hold it a minute. It feels heavy.

"I'll mow that lawn good," I tell her.

"I know you will," she says.

I dangle the money at Maude, and I want to jump up and shout over it. But Maude just looks dumb at it like it's a dream and she knows it.

"We got to go before it gets dark," I say, trying to keep the fire out of my voice so she won't know.

The old lady stands up. "I don't even have a flashlight to give you," she says.

"That's all right," I say. "I can see." I fold the money and put it in my pocket. I want to get out of there before she takes it back, so I take Maude's arm and pull her to the door. The old lady's pocketbook is sitting on the table and I glance back at it, wondering what else is in there.

"I'll come in the morning," I say.

"You're a good boy," she tells me again, and it stabs right through me. I open the door fast and we go out.

"Thanks for the pie," Maude tells her.

It's pretty dark, but we can see the path and the fence and the road. Maude hangs close to me as we stumble down the path. I keep one hand in my pocket, around the folded-up money.

When we get on the road it's even harder to see because we don't have the light from the house. A few stars are out, and a little chunk of moon is starting to get its glow.

"We can't go nowhere," Maude says. "We should go back."

But we keep going, down through them trees over-hanging the road so it's near to pitch black in there and we have to feel with our feet if we're on the road or not. It's the spookiest place I ever been, yet I'm not even that scared with the money in my pocket. I can feel by the way she holds on my shirt, though, that Maude is, but she just goes with me and don't ask no more questions.

About halfway down the road we come to a dead stop from the blackness. Trees block out the sky and there's nothing we can do but stand there.

"We gonna wait it out," I tell her.

"Here in the road?" she says.

I start shuffling us over to what's got to be the side of the road, and I'm holding her with one hand and waving my other arm out in front of me to feel the way. I touch branches.

"In here," I say. "Off the side."

We move into the woods a little ways, feeling for trees

and shrubs, stumbling over everything that's growing. I come up to a tree. "Right here," I say. "Sit down." And we feel our way down and sit there in the pitch black.

I can feel them woods full of living things, maybe in the trees too, who knows what's hanging over our heads. There's croaks and chirps and moving sounds. I'm straining to make sure the sounds are from what lives there and not from Pa sneaking around looking for us. I am blinking, trying to see, but there ain't no seeing.

"We gonna sleep here?" Maude says.

"We gonna try."

"Then what?" she says.

"Then I'm gonna find them underground tunnels so we can get. You heard that old lady. They go all the way to Georgia. Even to Florida."

I touch the outside of my pocket and feel the lump of folded-up money in there.

"Ain't you gonna mow that lady's lawn?" she says.

"I don't know," I tell her. I'm wondering if we go back would she trick us and call the police to take us, or would she give me the rest of the money like she said, and would it be one dollar or another twenty.

"Why'd she give you all that money?" Maude says.

" 'Cause she's a blind old bat," I tell her. But I don't know if that's why.

Then we're quiet, listening to what's out there in the woods making sounds. My insides go all hollow on me, like I'm floating out in the middle of nowhere, with no land underneath me and no way home. I see a picture of Pa crashing down the shades, and her sitting there in the chair with her big fat face after what she done and it's like I never lived in that house and never had no sisters but this one. It's like I never lived nowhere.

I look up but don't see nothing for the trees. I know there's stars out there, though, and that piece of moon, even if I can't see them. Maude settles back into the tree. "That pie was good," she mumbles.

I touch the money that lady give me. I don't know what I'm gonna do in the morning, go back to her house or head straight for them tunnels. Maybe there's an old railroad car left down there we can get into. Maybe there's things people left we can use.

I hear a sound and jump to, but it's only crickets out there. After a while I ease back against the tree and listen to them, and to Maude breathing.

I'm free, I think, free as that boy riding in the car with the radio and the cigarette, free as anybody. I can feel them tunnels under me, running through the hills like a good road to somewhere.

ABOUT THE AUTHOR

Mary Bush was born and grew up in Canastota, New York. She received a B.A. in English from the State University of New York at Buffalo, and an M.A. and D.A. in Syracuse University's graduate program in creative writing, where she worked with George Elliott and Raymond Carver. She is the co-founder, along with poet and novelist Rachel Guido DeVries, of the Community Writers' Project in Syracuse, where she is still listed as an affiliated writer. In 1985 she won the PEN/Nelson Algren award for the best unfinished collection of stories, several of which are included in this collection. She is an instructor in creative writing, composition, and literature at Hamilton College, New York.